THE GIRLS' BOOK OF SECRETS

piercey

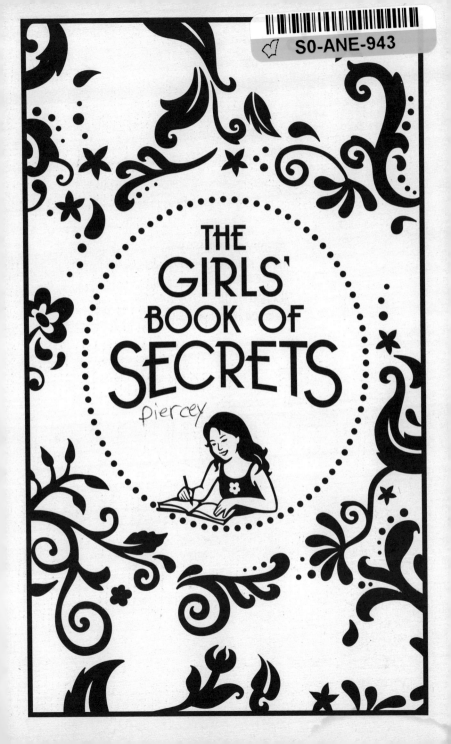

Written by Ellen Bailey
Illustrated by Nellie Ryan

Edited by Liz Scoggins
Designed by Angie Allison

THE GIRLS' BOOK OF SECRETS

SCHOLASTIC INC.
New York   Toronto   London   Auckland
Sydney   Mexico City   New Delhi   Hong Kong

NOTE TO READERS

ISBN 978-0-545-37356-2

First published as *The Yearbook for Girls* in Great Britain in 2010 by Buster Books, an imprint of Michael O'Mara Books Limited.

Text and illustrations copyright © Buster Books 2010
Cover design by Angie Allison
Cover illustration by Nellie Ryan

12 11 10 9 8 7 6 5 4 3 2 1   11 12 13 14 15 16/0

Printed in the U.S.A.   40
First American edition, July 2011

CONTENTS

GETTING STARTED

This book is about to change your life. Inside, you will find tons of quizzes and questions that will make you think and make you laugh. As you fill in the blank spaces, you'll be making a record of exactly who you are this year. Treasure it forever.

You don't have to read this book in any particular order, as each section you fill in has a space to make a note of the date, time, and place, like this:

Date .... Time .... Place ....

Each time there's a quiz or questionnaire, you'll need to fill out your opinion along the dotted line:

like this
....

or check the circle next to the answer you most agree with, like this:

Yes ✓ No ○

MEMORY BOX MEMENTOS

Follow the instructions on pages 10-12 to make a Memory Box. Use it to store all sorts of things, from **Memory Box Memento** suggestions throughout this book to ideas of your own. When this book is complete, store it in the Memory Box, too, so you'll know just where to look to remember this incredible year.

THIS BOOK IS ALL ABOUT ME

My name is ....

My nickname is ....

My birthday is on ....

I was born in the year ....

I live in ....

My star sign is ....

Right now I'm .... years old

I got this book on ....

My mom's name is ....

My dad's name is ....

I have .... brothers and .... sisters

Their names are ....

....

My school is called ....

My best friend is ....

I have .... pets

Signed ....

MAKING YOUR MEMORY BOX

Your Memory Box will be the perfect place to keep all sorts of treasured mementos that you can look back at in the future. It's simple to make – just follow the instructions below. First, think about the kind of style you want to create when decorating your Memory Box. Choose gift wrap with a vintage pattern, such as Victorian flowers for a classic feel, shiny metallics to create a futuristic style, or an up-to-date pattern to reflect the current year.

You will need:

• a cardboard box with a lid (a shoebox is perfect) • patterned gift wrap • plain gift wrap • a ruler • a pencil • scissors • a glue stick • craft glue • ribbon • a selection of sequins and buttons

1. On the back of the plain gift wrap, draw a rectangle that measures the same as the width and height of your box. Add 1 inch extra along the top and bottom, to fold around the top edge and onto the base of the box.

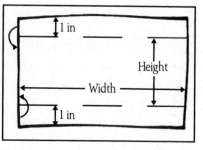

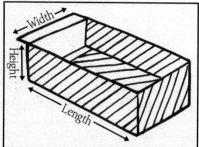

2. Draw another rectangle, exactly the same as the first, and cut them both out. Use your glue stick to glue one to the inside of each end of the box, as shown here.

3. Now draw another rectangle to line the base and the two long sides of the box. It should measure the same as the length of the box by the width and two times the height. Remember to add 1 inch extra at each end to overlap the edges.

4. Add a layer of glue all over the base and the two long sides, then stick this strip in place.

5. Next, lay your patterned gift wrap, right-side down, on a flat surface. Place the box on top and draw around the base. Add 1 inch extra on each side to fold around the sides of the box.

6. Glue this rectangle to the bottom of the box and stick the edges onto the sides.

7. Now measure a strip of the patterned gift wrap to cover all four sides. You may need to do this in two pieces if your paper is not long enough. Neatly glue the strip to the sides of the box.

8. Cover the lid in the same way.

9. Take another piece of plain gift wrap. On the back, write the words "Memory Box" backward in large bubble letters, like this:

XOᗺ YЯOMƎM

10. Carefully cut out the letters and glue them onto the lid of the box. Get an adult to help you cut out the centers of the letters if you need to, as this bit can be quite tricky.

11. Last of all, decorate the lid and the sides of the box with your selection of sequins, buttons, and glitter. Arrange them in a pattern you like, then use a dab of craft glue to secure each one.

12. Once the glue has dried thoroughly, tie your length of ribbon around the box in a bow to keep the lid secure.

Put your Memory Box in a safe place, such as the bottom of your closet. Pop any items that you'd like to keep in it, as well as any ideas you like from the **Memory Box Memento** suggestions in this book.

RIGHT HERE, RIGHT NOW

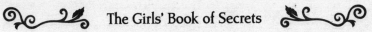

❧ Date ....

Time ....

Place .... ❧

Use this page to make a record of what you are doing at this exact moment in time.

What sounds can you hear right now?

....

What are you wearing? ....

....

How have you done your hair? ....

....

Who are you with? ....

What is the weather like? ....

....

What can you see right now? ....

....

What's in your pocket? ....

TAKING YOUR MEASUREMENTS

❧ Date .... Time .... Place .... ❧

Fill in your answers below, using whichever units of measurement you prefer – for instance, you can measure your height in feet and inches or in meters and centimeters.

Height. How tall are you? ....

How tall would you like to be? ....

Eyes. Most people say their eyes are blue, brown, green, or hazel. However, if you take a close look in the mirror you'll see flecks of all sorts of other colors in your irises – the colored part of your eye. Use a set of colored pencils in the picture below to show how many colors you can really see.

Hands. Spread your fingers out as wide as they can go. What is the distance from the tip of your thumb to the tip of your little finger?

....

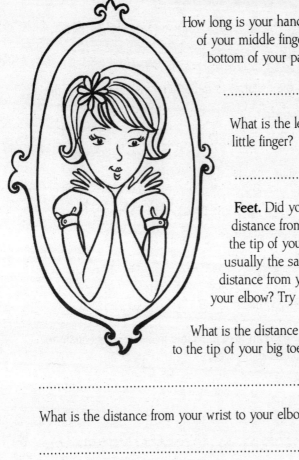

How long is your hand from the tip of your middle finger to the bottom of your palm?

....

What is the length of your little finger?

....

Feet. Did you know that the distance from your heel to the tip of your big toe is usually the same as the distance from your wrist to your elbow? Try it to see.

What is the distance from your heel to the tip of your big toe?

....

What is the distance from your wrist to your elbow?

....

Are both your feet exactly the same length? Yes ( ) No ( )

What color would you most like to paint your toes? Use colored pencils to decorate this set of nails.

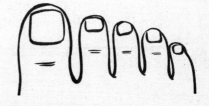

Ears. How long are your ears? ....

Is one higher than the other? Yes ⬭ No ⬭

Nose. What is the distance from between your eyes to the tip of your nose?

....

Do you think your nose is:

Too big ⬭ Too small ⬭ Just right ⬭ ?

Hair. How long is a strand of your hair?

....

How long would you like it to be? ....

In years to come, you can take the same measurements again to see how much you have changed.

Memory Box Memento. Next time you visit the hairdresser, keep a lock of your hair. Tie a length of thread around it to keep it together, then find a small box or envelope to put it in and pop it in your Memory Box.

LOOK TO THE FUTURE

Date .... Time .... Place ....

In ten years' time I want to

live in ....with

.... My pet will be a

.... named .... I want to be able to

.... My greatest achievement will

be ....

I will have met .... in real life.

My most treasured possession will be my

....

WHAT WILL BE, WILL BE

❧ Date .... Time .... Place .... ❧

What do you think the future will be like? What things do you think will be more popular, and what do you think will be less popular? Perhaps you think that recycling will be going up, and cars will be going down. Or maybe dogs will be going up, and cats will be going down? Fill the arrows below with your predictions.

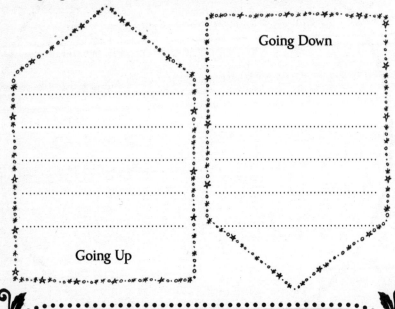

Going Down

....

....

....

....

....

Going Up

Memory Box Memento. Cut pictures out of magazines of things that you want to have in the future, such as a cool car or a big house. Stick them on a piece of paper to make a collage. Add decorations and words from the magazines, too.

YOUR EGYPTIAN HOROSCOPE

Date .... Time .... Place ....

You're probably familiar with the kind of horoscopes that appear every day in newspapers. You might even know your Chinese horoscope, based on the year of your birth, but you may not have come across many Egyptian horoscopes before.

The ancient Egyptians believed that the exact position of the stars on the day you were born would affect your destiny and give you characteristics of the god whose sign you were born under. Here's what a horoscope might have been like at the time of the pharaohs. What does your Egyptian horoscope say about you?

Thoth – god of learning
August 29 – September 27

People born under Thoth are usually clever and good at solving problems. You love organizing fun activities for your friends and you're spontaneous and full of original ideas.

Horus – god of the sky
September 28–October 27

If you were born under Horus, you are likely to have great ambitions that you'll need to work hard to achieve. You are also brave, sociable, motivated, and outgoing.

Wadjet – protector goddess
October 28–November 26

You are loyal and unselfish, and always stand up for your friends. You tend to approach new things with caution and think them through clearly first.

Sekhmet – goddess of war
November 27–December 26

You are likely to be fiercely intelligent. Your friends love your brilliant sense of humor and that you can remain optimistic through tough times. You are imaginative and energetic.

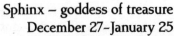

Sphinx – goddess of treasure
December 27–January 25

Those born under this sign can often adapt to any situation. You're good at keeping secrets and your friends aren't afraid to share their problems with you. You are also tidy, organized, and intelligent.

Shu – god of air
January 26–February 24

People born under Shu are often very creative. You are good at sorting out problems between your friends and hate seeing people upset. You are fair, kind, and have a good sense of humor.

Isis – goddess of mothers
February 25–March 26

People born under Isis are usually excellent listeners. You make friends easily and don't judge people. You are trustworthy, straightforward, and reliable.

Osiris – god of the afterlife
March 27–April 25

You are brilliant at coming up with new and exciting ideas. Your friends love your sense of adventure. You are intelligent and lively, so nothing is ever dull when you're around.

Amun – god of creation
April 26–May 25

If you were born under this sign, you are likely to be strong and brave. Your confidence makes you a born leader and your friends often come to you for advice.

Hathor – goddess of music, dance, and joy
May 26–June 24

People born under the sign of Hathor have a serious romantic streak. As well as being emotional and passionate, you are likely to be popular and have lots of close friends.

Phoenix – bird-god of new life
June 25–July 24

If you were born under this sign, you are especially
good at turning difficult situations into wonderful
new beginnings. Your friends love your sunny
personality and upbeat, optimistic nature.

Anubis – guardian-god of the dead
July 25–August 28

People born under Anubis are likely to be protectors
who look after people. Your friends admire your
confidence and determination. You are generous
and kind, and never give up.

Memory Box Memento. First, read what your Egyptian
horoscope says about you. Then take a piece of paper and
write your own predictions for what might happen to you in
the future. Imagine what subjects you might choose to study,
who you will go out with when you're older, where you might
live, and so on. Seal your predictions inside an envelope and
write on the date you are allowed to open it in the future. Tuck
it away at the bottom of your Memory Box, but don't forget to
check if your predictions came true.

TEN THINGS TO ACHIEVE THIS YEAR

❧ Date .... Time .... Place .... ❧

Try to achieve each of these ideas within the year and check each one off as soon as you manage it. If there is something you particularly want to try that isn't on the list, make a note of it at the bottom of the page and check it off once you have succeeded, too.

Raise some money for charity ○

Laugh so hard my sides hurt ○

Grow a plant from seed ○

Master a recipe ○

Make at least one new friend ○

Visit a place I've never been to before ○

Make someone a birthday present from scratch ○

Perform something in public ○

Overcome one of my fears ○

Start keeping a journal ○

....

.... ○

MOOD CALCULATOR

❧ Date .... Time .... Place .... ❧

Use this section to unload anything you like.

Is anything annoying you right now? Yes ◯ No ◯

If yes, what is it? ....

....

....

What are you happiest about right now?

....

....

Are you worried about anything? Yes ◯ No ◯

If yes, what is it? ....

....

Who did you last argue with?

....

What about? ....

Have you made up yet? Yes ◯ No ◯

MIRROR, MIRROR

Date .... Time .... Place ....

Draw a picture of yourself in the mirror below, then write four words that describe how you're feeling today around the outside.

....

....

....

....

TEN THINGS TO STOP WORRYING ABOUT THIS YEAR

Date .... Time .... Place ....

This year, why not make a resolution (a promise to yourself) to worry less? Think of all the things that are most likely to make you bite your nails or chew your lip. List them in order, so that the most worrying thing is at number one. Once you've written things down, they'll probably seem less worrying already.

1. ....

2. ....

3. ....

4. ....

5. ....

6. ....

7. ....

8. ....

9. ....

10. ....

THAT'S SO ANNOYING!

 Date .... Time .... Place ....

Write down four things that really annoy you in the top row, such as bees or people kicking the back of your chair. Choose which thing from each pair is more annoying, then decide which of the final two is the thing that annoys you the most.

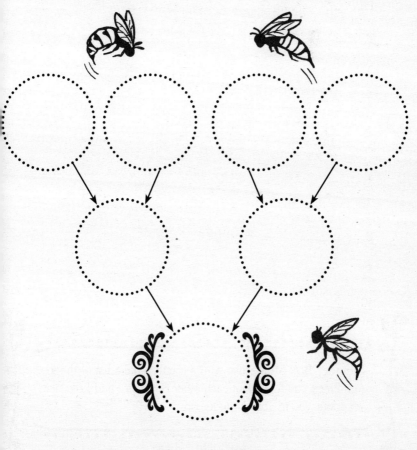

TOP TEN THINGS I LIKE ABOUT ME

Date .... Time .... Place ....

Organize the ten things you like most about yourself into a top ten list, according to how you rate each point, with the best at number one.

1. ....

2. ....

3. ....

4. ....

5. ....

6. ....

7. ....

8. ....

9. ....

10. ....

Memory Box Memento. With a friend, write a list of the top ten things you like about each other. Swap lists and keep her list about you in your Memory Box.

SUPERFAN OR SUPERSTAR?

❧ Date .... Time .... Place .... ❧

Do you think you're more likely to become a superstar or a superfan? It's time to make up your mind – study each option and check your preference.

Shop online ◌	Personal shopper ◌
Fish sticks ◌	Oysters ◌
Photographer ◌	Model ◌
Take out ◌	Restaurant ◌
Milk chocolate ◌	Dark chocolate ◌
Roadie ◌	Lead singer ◌
Shower ◌	Bubble bath ◌
Sneakers ◌	High heels ◌
Autograph hunter ◌	Autograph signer ◌
Good friends ◌	Entourage ◌
Kitten ◌	Lapdog ◌
Minivan ◌	Tour bus ◌

ALL IN A NIGHT'S SLEEP

❧ Date .... Time .... Place .... ❧

Complete this questionnaire to record your sleeping habits.

✿ Do you share your bedroom? Yes ◯ No ◯

✿ If yes, who with? ....

✿ Blankets ◯ ? Comforter ◯ ?

✿ What color? ....

✿ What time do you normally go to bed? ....

✿ How many hours of sleep do you normally get each night?

.... hours.

✿ How long do you brush your teeth for?

.... minutes .... seconds

✿ Floss ◯ ? Mouthwash ◯ ?

✿ What do you wear to bed? ....

....

✿ Do you read for a while ◯ ? Watch TV for a while ◯ ?

✿ Do you leave the door open ◯ ? Leave the window open ◯ ?

❀ Do you sleep:

On your side ⬭ On your back ⬭ On your front ⬭ ?

❀ When you wake up in the morning does your bedding look like:

You've fought a monster ⬭ ?

You've slept perfectly still, like Sleeping Beauty ⬭ ?

Somewhere in between these two things ⬭ ?

❀ Have you ever:

Fallen out of bed ⬭ ?

Woken up with your feet at the pillow end ⬭ ?

Wriggled so much that your sheets came off in the night ⬭ ?

SWEET DREAMS

✤ Date .... Time .... Place .... ✤

Anything is possible in dreams. Think of your five favorites and write them out in order, so that the best dream is number one.

1. ....
   ....

2. ....
   ....

3. ....
   ....

4. ....
   ....

5. ....
   ....

Memory Box Memento. Make a record of a week in your dreams. Cut two sheets of paper into quarters. Write the date and describe each night's dream on each card. Draw a picture of the dream on the back then punch a hole in the top left-hand corner. Tie them together with a length of pretty ribbon.

FUNNIEST THINGS OF ALL TIME

❧ Date .... Time .... Place .... ❧

Think of the ten funniest things that have ever happened to you, that you've seen in a movie or on TV, or your favorite jokes. Organize them into a top ten list, with your favorite at number one.

1. ....

2. ....

3. ....

4. ....

5. ....

6. ....

7. ....

8. ....

9. ....

....

10. ....

....

....

FASHION FAVORITES

❧ Date .... Time .... Place .... ❧

Check your favorite item from each category below, then draw your favorite outfit on the mannequin opposite.

Necklines. Halter ◯ V-neck ◯ Square ◯ Round ◯

Hats. Beret ◯ Baseball cap ◯ Straw hat ◯ Ski cap ◯

Fabrics. Silk ◯ Cotton ◯ Denim ◯ Wool ◯

Jewelry. Sparkly ◯ Wooden ◯ Gold ◯ Silver ◯

Shopping. Internet ◯ Thrift ◯ Mall ◯ Boutique ◯

Shoes. Flip-flops ◯ Sneakers ◯ High heels ◯ Flats ◯

Bags. Beach ◯ Clutch ◯ Backpack ◯ Woven ◯

Coats. Duffle ◯ Denim ◯ Waterproof ◯ Leather ◯

Clothing. Casual ◯ Designer ◯ Vintage ◯ Homemade ◯

Style. Urban ◯ Sporty ◯ Romantic ◯ Preppy ◯

Prints. Bright ◯ Flowery ◯ Animal ◯ Geometric ◯

Jeans. Skinny ◯ Flared ◯ Baggy ◯ Boot-cut ◯

Warmth. Cardigan ◯ Shawl ◯ Hoodie ◯ Scarf ◯

In bed. Pajamas ◯ T-shirt ◯ Nightie ◯ Tank and shorts ◯

Inspiration. Friends ◯ Celebs ◯ Ads ◯ Music ◯

MY FAVORITE OUTFIT

Choose items of clothing you already own or pieces that you'd just love to have to complete your perfect outfit.

Use the space around the mannequin to describe the fabrics and what the outfit is for, or even to draw patterns or describe textures in more detail.

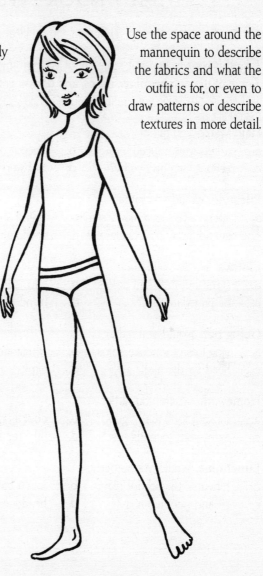

WHAT'S YOUR STYLE?

❧ Date .... Time .... Place .... ❧

Take this quiz to find out more about yourself and your style. Make a note of the number of **a**s, **b**s, **c**s, and **d**s you get as you go along and check out what your results mean on page 38. Here goes . . .

Hair. Would you rather . . .
a. . . . it gets you noticed?   **b.** . . . keep it out of the way?
c. . . . keep it long and shiny?   **d.** . . . not worry about it at all?

Lifestyle. Would you rather . . .
a. . . . spend a day as a movie star? **b.** . . . spend a day as an athlete?
c. . . . spend a day as a designer?   **d.** . . . spend a day as a professor?

Clothes. Would you rather . . .
a. . . . stand out in bright colors? **b.** . . . have sneakers at the ready?
c. . . . be pretty in pink?   **d.** . . . blend into the background?

Going out. Would you rather . . .
a. . . . sing lots of karaoke solos? **b.** . . . whizz around in a go-kart?
c. . . . head for the mall?   **d.** . . . explore a museum?

Homework. Would you rather . . .
a. . . . make it look really good?   **b.** . . . do it as quickly as you can?
c. . . . paint your toenails first?   **d.** . . . take time to do it well?

Lunchtime. Would you rather . . .
a. . . . rehearse the school play?   **b.** . . . join a game of soccer?
c. . . . sit and people-watch?   **d.** . . . head for the library?

Evenings. Would you rather . . .
a. . . . plan tomorrow's outfit? **b.** . . . play a sport?
c. . . . try out a new hairstyle? **d.** . . . watch a documentary?

Friends. Would you rather be . . .
a. . . . leader of the pack? **b.** . . . friends with the whole team?
c. . . . one of the girls? **d.** . . . best friends forever?

Superstar. Would you rather . . .
a. . . . have star quality? **b.** . . . be faster than anyone else?
c. . . . be completely glamorous? **d.** . . . be a total genius?

The future. Would you rather . . .
a. . . . become a pop star? **b.** . . . make the Olympic team?
c. . . . become super-rich? **d.** . . . win a Nobel Prize?

Away from home. Would you rather . . .
a. . . . go to drama camp? **b.** . . . go on an adventure vacation?
c. . . . lie in the sun? **d.** . . . take in the city sights?

If you were a boy! Would you rather . . .
a. . . . be lead singer in a band? **b.** . . . join the football team?
c. . . . style your hair all day? **d.** . . . spend the day studying?

YOUR STYLE ANSWERS

(Mostly **a**s.) **Fun and flamboyant.** You have plenty of confidence and don't mind standing out from the crowd. You might surprise a lot of people with your softer side, so don't forget to let it show sometimes.

(Mostly **b**s.) **Sporty star.** You have tons of energy and can't help but be outgoing. You love to try new things, and make friends easily. Don't forget to take a break every now and then, to give yourself the chance to relax.

(Mostly **c**s.) **Party princess.** You love to spend time on your appearance, and enjoy being pampered. That doesn't mean you don't have a serious side, and you'll often surprise your friends and family with your clever and witty observations.

(Mostly **d**s.) **Ahead of the game.** You're very organized and usually like to make sure you're on top of things. Your parents and teachers probably appreciate how hard you study. Although you like to look before you leap, remember to save time to have fun with friends.

PRINCE CHARMING

❧ Date .... Time .... Place .... ❧

Ever wondered how you'll recognize your Prince Charming when he comes along? Rank the personality qualities below from 1–5, so you know exactly what you're looking for in the perfect partner.

Not Important ←— 1　　2　　3　　4　　5 —→ Really important

Funny　　◯◯◯◯◯

Confident　　◯◯◯◯◯

Intelligent　　◯◯◯◯◯

Mature　　◯◯◯◯◯

Practical　　◯◯◯◯◯

Cool　　◯◯◯◯◯

Ambitious　　◯◯◯◯◯

Enthusiastic　　◯◯◯◯◯

Modest　　◯◯◯◯◯

Sensitive　　◯◯◯◯◯

Easy-going　　◯◯◯◯◯

Independent　　◯◯◯◯◯

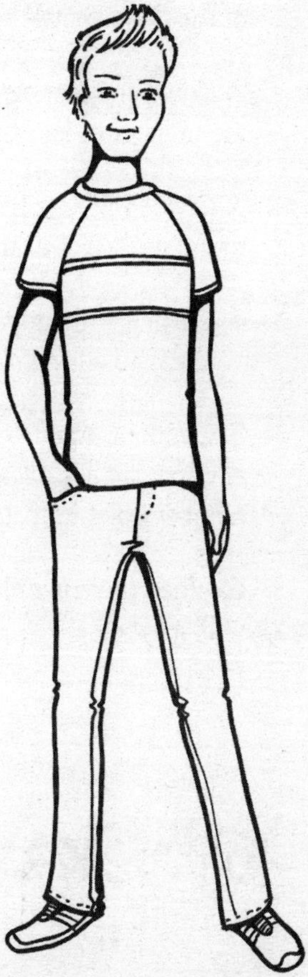

WHICH BOY IS RIGHT FOR ME?

Date .... Time .... Place ....

Have you ever wondered which boy you might be destined to go out with in the future? Work it out using the steps below.

1. First, write different boys' names that you already know in each of the flower petals on the opposite page.

2. Count the number of letters in your first name, and add it to the number of letters in your last name.

3. Divide this number by two. If you end up with a half number, round it up. (For example, if you get 5.5, round it up to 6).

4. Starting at the top petal, count around the flower petals until you reach your number, then color in that petal.

5. Continue counting on the following uncolored petals, skipping any that are already colored in. Every time you reach your number, color in that petal.

6. When there is only one petal left uncolored, that's your boy – well, maybe!

Memory Box Memento. If you have one, pop a photo of your favorite boy into your Memory Box. To remind yourself what you like about him, describe his best qualities on the back and any favorite moments you have shared. If you haven't met him yet, write where you would go on an ideal first date.

BOYS — FRIENDS OR FOES?

❧ Date .... Time .... Place .... ❧

Ask your friends to suggest ten boys for you. Write each name in one of the spaces below. Think about each boy and decide whether you would be friends, foes, or love him forever. "Undecided" is not an option.

	Friend	Foe	Forever
❀	◯	◯	◯
❀	◯	◯	◯
❀	◯	◯	◯
❀	◯	◯	◯
❀	◯	◯	◯
❀	◯	◯	◯
❀	◯	◯	◯
❀	◯	◯	◯
❀	◯	◯	◯
❀	◯	◯	◯

LOVE IT, HATE IT

 Date .... Time .... Place ....

Color in the hearts below. Use pink if you love what's written inside the heart, blue if you hate it, and yellow if you don't feel strongly either way.

Going to the movies

Boys

Shopping

Being neat and tidy

Karaoke

Spicy food

Horoscopes

Camping

Chatting with
friends

Carnival
rides

BEST NAMES EVER

❧ Date .... Time .... Place .... ❧

List your ten favorite girls' names and your ten favorite boys' names. Organize each list into a top ten, according to how much you love them, so that your favorites are number one.

Girls' Names	Boys' Names
1.	1. ....
2.	2. ....
3.	3. ....
4.	4. ....
5.	5. ....
6.	6. ....
7.	7. ....
8.	8. ....
9.	9. ....
10.	10. ....

Is your own name on the list? Yes ◯ No ◯

Would you change it to your favorite if you could? Yes ◯ No ◯

SCHOOL DAYS

❧ Date .... Time .... Place .... ❧

People often say that school days are the best days of your life, but what really goes on at your school?

❀ I love it at school when ....

❀ I hate it at school when ....

❀ My school uniform is okay ◌ awful ◌ I don't have one ◌

❀ The best school trip I've ever been on was to ....

....

❀ My favorite subject is ....

❀ The funniest person in my class is ....

❀ My favorite teacher is ....

❀ I last got in trouble because I ....

....

❀ My best excuse for being late is ....

....

❀ I eat lunch with ....

❀ At recess, I like to ....

CAREER DAY

Date .... Time .... Place ....

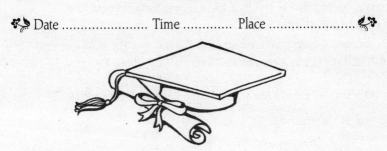

Answer these questions to discover your career destiny. As you go along, make a note of each time you answer **a**, **b**, **c**, or **d**. Then turn to page 49 for your results.

❀ From the following subjects, which is your favorite?

   a. Art.
   b. P.E.
   c. Drama.
   d. Science.

❀ Which of these vacations would you prefer?

   a. Relaxing in a beautiful beach house.
   b. Camping somewhere with stunning scenery.
   c. Staying at a hotel in a stylish, fast-paced city.
   d. Visiting amazing ancient buildings in distant locations.

❀ What are you most likely to be in charge of in a group project?

   a. Drawing illustrations and creating charts.
   b. Presenting the project to the class at the end.
   c. Taking the lead and managing the project.
   d. Researching the project and providing the key facts.

❀How would you help your best friend celebrate her birthday?

   a. Invite a few of her best friends over for a sleepover.
   b. Arrange a big picnic in the park.
   c. Invite everyone she knows to the party of the year.
   d. Take her to a movie she's been talking about for ages.

❀If you were an animal, which would you be?

   a. A chimpanzee.
   b. A horse.
   c. A kitten.
   d. A lion.

❀Which of the following would you most like to win?

   a. The Nobel Peace Prize.
   b. A gold medal at the Olympics.
   c. People's Choice Award.
   d. The Women in Science award.

❀Which of these desserts would you most like to eat?

   a. A big chocolate brownie.
   b. An ice pop.
   c. A banana split.
   d. A strawberry tart.

❀Which of the following gifts would you most like to receive?

   a. A playlist put together by your best friend.
   b. A trip to a theme park.
   c. A new cell phone.
   d. A video game.

CAREER-DAY ANSWERS

(Mostly **a**s.) **People person.** Thoughtful and creative – you'd make a great interior designer, illustrator, or novelist. Any career working with people would be ideal, too – perhaps as a teacher, a therapist, or a nurse.

(Mostly **b**s.) **Outdoor girl.** You love rolling up your sleeves. A job as a nature conservationist would be perfect, but you could also consider becoming a landscape gardener, a set designer, or a journalist.

(Mostly **c**s.) **Celeb-in-waiting.** Of all the personality types, you're the most likely to become famous. You love to plan outings, so you'd be amazing at public relations (organizing events such as book launches, restaurant openings, and press conferences). You could even work as a TV presenter or host your own radio show.

(Mostly **d**s.) **High-flier.** You know your own mind and aren't afraid to study hard to make your dreams come true. You're destined for a career that makes lots of money and will earn you respect. A career as a doctor, architect, lawyer, or banker would be perfect for you.

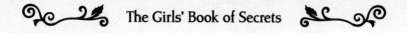

MOST LIKELY TO . . .

❧ Date .... Time .... Place .... ☙

It's time to nominate your favorite people for a set of very special prizes. Do you have a friend who's always one step ahead of the latest trend and is bound to become a fashion icon? Or perhaps you have a relative who loves to be the center of attention and is sure to end up on television?

In each of these frames, draw a picture or glue a photo of the person you think should receive each of the awards listed below. Don't forget to write the name underneath each portrait.

Who is most likely to . . .

... win a Nobel Prize?   ... appear on TV?

... get detention?   ... become a millionaire?

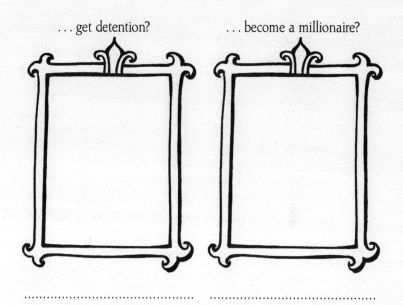

....

... run a marathon?   ... write a novel?

....

... break a bone?

... publish their memoirs?

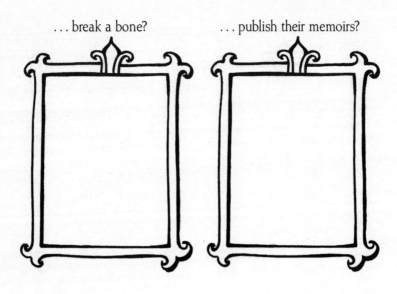

... work with animals?

... become a fashion icon?

... trip on the red carpet?

....

... raise their hand in class?

....

UNDER PRESSURE

🌿 Date ....

Time .... Place .... 🌸

In a difficult situation, are you as cool as a cucumber or as wobbly as jelly? Answer these questions, and make a note of the number of **a**s, **b**s, **c**s, and **d**s you get. Then turn to page 57 to find out your results.

❀ On a Friday afternoon, your teacher announces that everyone must present a project to the class on Monday. How does this make you feel?

a. Your heart starts pounding and your hands feel sweaty – you'll have to pretend to be sick.
b. Eek! That sounds scary, but you know that if you work hard on it all weekend it'll be okay.
c. No problem – you've got a great idea for the project and know you'll get a good grade.
d. You certainly won't spend any time worrying about it – you'll just tell a few jokes and hope for the best.

❀ Your dad is driving you to meet your friends at the movies when the car breaks down. How do you react?

a. Complain to him for making you miss out and sulk all night.
b. Ask him to let you take the bus instead.

c. Text your friends to ask them to wait until the next showing.
d. Go for a burger with your dad instead.

❀ On a bowling trip with your family, your parents say they'll give a money prize to the winner. How do you perform?

a. You try hard, but don't enjoy it as much because you're focused on winning the money.
b. You wish your parents hadn't made it into a competition, but try your hardest to win.
c. It's no problem – the money's yours!
d. You cheat by distracting everyone else when it's their turn to bowl.

❀ You and your friends are competing in a karaoke contest. What happens when it's your turn?

a. You run and hide until everyone's forgotten that it was your turn.
b. You start off a bit shaky, but soon get into it.
c. You do a dazzling performance with a few added dance moves.
d. You show off your talent for burping songs.

❀ A friend tells you that a boy in your class likes you. You like him too, so what do you do?

a. You avoid looking him in the eye and go red when he talks to you.
b. You don't do anything, but hope he asks you out.
c. You smile and talk to him whenever you see him.
d. You make fun of him.

❀ Your friends are making up a dance for the school talent show. How would you help?

a. Offer to design outfits so that you don't have to go onstage.
b. Let your best friend come up with most of the moves – she's a great dancer.
c. Choreograph the routine so that you're sure to win.
d. You think talent shows are silly and wouldn't help.

❀ You've got an exam tomorrow, but your little sister and her friend are distracting you from studying. How do you react?

a. Yell at them about how important it is that you get your work done.
b. Ask them to go and play in another room.
c. Join in for half an hour and then go back to your studies.
d. Teach them a new game – you weren't really studying anyway.

❀ Your friends are coming over for your birthday and you've baked a cake. The bad news is that you left it in the oven too long and it's burned! What do you do?

a. Call all your friends and cancel the party. It's ruined.
b. Be so upset that your mom agrees to make a new one for you.
c. Run to the local store to pick up a ready-made cake.
d. Feed your friends sandwiches instead of birthday cake.

UNDER-PRESSURE ANSWERS

(Mostly **a**s.) **Stress head.** You often feel anxious and find it difficult to cope in some situations. You sometimes take this out on other people, and your friends know to keep out of your way if you're in a bad mood. Don't be too hard on yourself – take some time out every now and again to relax.

(Mostly **b**s.) **Worry bunny.** You don't like being under pressure to perform, but you've developed ways of dealing with it. You like to prepare for situations that you know are going to be stressful, and do a good job. However, if things don't go to plan, you can get upset. Try not to worry so much, and don't be afraid to make a bit of a fool of yourself.

(Mostly **c**s.) **Cool cat.** You're super-confident and relaxed in most situations. You work hard and have a great attitude, but not everyone's as confident as you. Remember not to push people into situations that they might feel uncomfortable in.

(Mostly **d**s.) **Class clown.** People think you're strong and confident, but actually there are lots of situations that you find scary. You cover this up by making jokes or pretending you don't care, and this can hurt people's feelings. Try to let your friends know when you feel this way – you'll be surprised by how understanding they are.

FREE-TIME FAVORITES

❧ Date .... Time .... Place .... ❧

If you had to choose, how would you most like to spend your free time? Pick just one option from each activity below that you prefer to the other three, then underline your absolute favorite activity.

Movies. Comedy ◯ Action ◯ Romance ◯ Scary ◯

Music. Pop ◯ Rock ◯ R&B ◯ Classical ◯

Pampering. Manicure ◯ Pedicure ◯ Facial ◯ Hairstyling ◯

Reading. Novels ◯ Magazines ◯ Texts ◯ Comics ◯

Culture. Museum ◯ Theater ◯ Concert ◯ Gallery ◯

Exercise. Swimming ◯ Running ◯ Yoga ◯ Aerobics ◯

After-school club. Music ◯ Dance ◯ Drama ◯ Sports ◯

TV. Cartoons ◯ Soaps ◯ Sitcoms ◯ Reality shows ◯

Day trip. Zoo ◯ Aquarium ◯ Water park ◯ Theme park ◯

At home. Cooking ◯ Sewing ◯ Gardening ◯ Sleeping ◯

Getting around. Bike ◯ Skateboard ◯ Walk ◯ Scooter ◯

At the beach. Snorkel ◯ Surf ◯ Sunbathe ◯ Sandcastles ◯

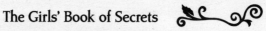

TV ADDICT

❧ Date .... Time .... Place .... ❧

Think of your ten favorite television programs, then organize your list into a top ten, according to how much you really enjoy them. Your favorite should be number one.

1. ....
2. ....
3. ....
4. ....
5. ....
6. ....
7. ....
8. ....
9. ....
10. ....

BEST BOOKS OF ALL TIME

❧ Date .... Time .... Place .... ❧

Organize the books that you like most into a top ten list, according to how much you enjoyed them and how memorable they are, with the title of the book that you think is best at number one.

1. ....

2. ....

3. ....

4. ....

5. ....

6. ....

7. ....

8. ....
....

9. ....
....

10. ....

....

WHAT DO YOUR DOODLES DO?

❧ Date .... Time .... Place .... ❧

The way you write and draw can reveal a lot about your personality. Make your mark on the following three pages, then turn to pages 64 to 66 to discover what your doodling style says about you.

SIGNATURE STYLE

First, don't think about it too much, but just sign your name in the box below:

TIME TO WRITE

Now copy out the words, "This is what my writing looks like," below:

Now, turn the page and get doodling. . . .

CIRCLE OF TRUTH

Join the ends of this line, any way you like:

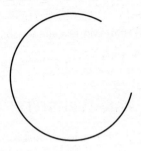

DO A DOODLE

Use this space to doodle the first thing that comes into your head.

COPYCAT

Now copy this spiral in the space on the right.

PIG PEN

Lastly, draw a picture of a pig here.

Now turn the page to find out what your writing and doodles say about you.

YOUR DOODLE ANSWERS

SIGNATURE STYLE

If your signature is large and fills the box, you're an outgoing girl who loves to be the centre of attention.

If your signature's small and there's lots of space around it you're a thoughtful girl who enjoys spending time on her own.

TIME TO WRITE

If your writing leans to the right *like this*, you're warm, caring and emotional. Your heart rules your head.

If your writing stands upright **like this**, you're good at keeping your emotions in check and have a balanced attitude.

If your writing leans to the left **like this**, you try to conceal your feelings from others. Your head rules your heart.

CIRCLE OF TRUTH

If you completed the circle like this, you're a conventional girl who values traditions. You're practical, sensible, and trustworthy.

If you completed the circle with zigzag lines, you have a strong sense of responsibility but also like to take the occasional risk.

If you turned the circle into something else completely, you're an imaginative, creative girl who hates being made to follow rules.

DO A DOODLE

Hearts and flowers. You're all about peace and love. You're caring, kind, and thoughtful.

Geometric shapes. You're a clear thinker – organized and good at planning.

Patterns. You have lots of energy and are always on the go. You're creative and good at paying attention to detail.

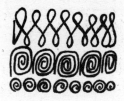

People and animals. You're a warm, friendly girl with a big heart. You dislike spending time on your own.

COPYCAT

If you started at the outside of the spiral and drew inward, you like to look at the big picture and think about the details afterward.

If you started at the inside of the spiral and drew outward, you like to focus on details before thinking about how they fit into the bigger plan.

PIG PEN

If the pig is facing to the left, you spend a lot of time thinking about the past. You have an excellent memory.

If the pig is facing forwards, you live in the present and appreciate each moment as it happens.

If the pig is facing to the right, you are always busy thinking about the future and what's going to happen next.

SCARIEST THINGS OF ALL TIME

❧ Date .... Time .... Place .... ❧

Everyone's fears are different, so the things that make your best friend squirm, scream, or shudder might be no sweat to you. Take a deep breath, grab a pen, and get checking – it's time to face your fears. Out of each group, which thing scares you the most?

❀ Slimy things ◯ Crawly things ◯

   Spiky things ◯ Sticky things ◯

❀ Science tests ◯ Math tests ◯

   History tests ◯ Spanish tests ◯

❀ Bungee jumping ◯ Scuba diving ◯

   Skydiving ◯ Whitewater rafting ◯

❀ Spiders ◯ Bats ◯ Snakes ◯ Rats ◯

❀ Lions ◯ Sharks ◯ Bears ◯ Wolves ◯

❀ Singing onstage ◯ Making a speech in public ◯

   Falling over at a dance ◯ No one knowing who you are ◯

❀ Graveyards ◯ Caves ◯ Cellars ◯ Attics ◯

❀ Ghosts ◯ Vampires ◯ Zombies ◯ Werewolves ◯

❀ Roller coasters ◯ Elevators ◯ Fast cars ◯ Airplanes ◯

FIGHT THE FEAR

Date .... Time .... Place ....

When it comes to the things that worry or frighten you most, your imagination can be a powerful tool. If something makes your heart pound and your stomach flutter with butterflies, there's a simple technique to help you conquer those fears, so find a quiet space and follow these steps:

1. First, sit and think about the thing that scares or worries you, and picture it as a bright ball of light inside you.

2. Now, imagine taking the ball of light out of your body, so that you can see it in front of you. Picture the ball turning into a creature or a character that you think suits it, for instance a spider made out of numbers if your fear is a math test.

3. Next, think of a hero that can challenge the fear. It could be a superhero, or a creature that is stronger than your fear. Imagine your hero next to your fear.

4. Now, visualize your hero fighting your fear. Perhaps she shoots fireballs at it, jumps up and down on it, or simply covers it in silly string. Imagine your hero beating your fear and winning the fight.

5. Next time you start to feel afraid, take a deep breath and remember your hero beating your fear. You could even show your fear character exactly what you think of it by drawing it on a tissue and flushing it down the toilet!

ARE YOU A MONEY MASTER?

❦ Date .... Time .... Place .... ❦

Make a note of the number of times you answer **a**, **b**, or **c** in this quiz, then turn to page 71 to discover if you control your money or if your money controls you!

❀ It's your best friend's birthday next week and you haven't bought her a present yet. Which would you decide to do?

a. Buy her the expensive shoes she's been wanting for months.

b. Make her something instead of buying it – homemade gifts show that you care, and you can make it more personal, too.

$100

c. Get together with some friends to buy her the shoes she loves from all of you.

❀ You see a great dress for the school dance in a store window. Which would you decide to do?

a. Go right in and buy it without even trying it on.
b. Look at the price tag before you do anything else.
c. Try it on, and make sure you can think of at least three different occasions on which you can wear it before you buy it.

❀ It's time to plan a family vacation. Would you:

a. Start thumbing through glossy vacation brochures immediately?
b. Dig out your tent and get ready for some camping fun?
c. Research online and shop around for the best deals?

❁ The latest issue of your favorite magazine is out. Would you:

a. Buy it immediately? It's got all the gossip on your favorite celebrities and you don't want to miss out.
b. Leave it on the shelf? You've been saving for ages, and you're sure you can find out the gossip from your friends anyway.
c. Go halves with your best friend? You can read it together and have fun sharing the stories.

❁ You and your friends go out for a nice lunch. Would you rather:

a. Order a full three-course meal – everything looks so delicious?
b. Go for the cheapest option on the menu?
c. Ask for tap water with your meal and suggest you go home for ice cream, instead of having an expensive dessert?

❁ You can't decide which of two bags to buy. Are you more likely to:

a. Buy them both – they'll both get used?
b. Buy the cheapest one?
c. Buy the one that goes with more of your outfits?

❁ Your friends are planning a trip to the movies. You really want to go, but can't afford it. Would you:

a. Borrow the money from your parents and go anyway? You'll just have to do more chores than usual to make up for it.
b. Tell your friends you can't make it and have a night in?
c. Invite everyone over for a DVD party at your house instead?

❁ Congratulations! You've won $50 in a competition. Will you:

a. Hit the stores the first chance you get?
b. Put it in the bank? It's sure to come in handy in the future.
c. Save some of it, but treat yourself to something new as well?

MONEY-MASTER ANSWERS

(Mostly **a**s.) **Shopaholic.** You really love to shop! However, learning to save money rather than splurging is a useful skill. Try to save a little each month, wait until your piggy bank is bulging, then reward yourself by using it to buy something really special.

(Mostly **b**s.) **Supersaver.** Thoughtful and cautious, you are very careful with your money and will rarely buy anything unless you really need it. It's important to spend wisely, but make sure you remember to treat yourself to something fun every once in a while.

(Mostly **c**s.) **Money master.** You keep an eye on your cash and make sure you don't spend too much, yet you're still able to buy the things you want by saving up for them. Keep up the good work.

MUSIC MIXES

❧ Date .... Time .... Place .... ❧

Whether you want to cheer yourself up, or just want to get in the
party spirit, music can have an amazing effect on your mood. Use
this space to list and order your favorite songs or pieces of music
for each category (add who each one is by, if you know).

RELAXING

1. ....

2. ....

3. ....

4. ....

5. ....

DANCING DIVA

1. ....

2. ....

3. ....

4. ....

5. ....

SAD AND SOULFUL

1. ....

2. ....

3. ....

4. ....

5. ....

OH-SO-ANNOYING

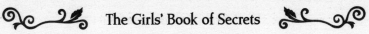

1. ....

....

2. ....

....

3. ....

....

4. ....

....

5. ....

....

FANTASY BAND ON TOUR

Date .... Time .... Place ....

Whether or not you play an instrument, anyone can have a successful fantasy band. First, you need to choose your bandmates and decide which role everyone should take within your band. Assign each role below to the friend you think it suits most.

❀ **Lead singer** ....

❀ **Lead guitarist** ....

❀ **Bass guitarist** ....

❀ **Drummer** ....

❀ **Keyboards** ....

❀ **Backup singer 1** ....

....

❀ **Backup singer 2** ....

....

....

❀ **Tour manager** ....

....

....

RECORDING STARS

Next, it's time to give your band a name. Circle your favorite word from each column below. Add them together to complete the name of your band. You might consider writing them out in an unusual way – for example, as one word, such as "Superblueflowers" – to make your fantasy band's name a bit different.

Party	Funk	Kittens
Cute	Green	Flowers
Pretty	Soul	Seeds
Super	Pink	Things
Girly	Rock	Singers
Crazy	Blue	Fliers

NAME THAT TUNE

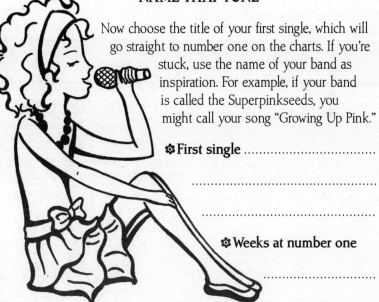

Now choose the title of your first single, which will go straight to number one on the charts. If you're stuck, use the name of your band as inspiration. For example, if your band is called the Superpinkseeds, you might call your song "Growing Up Pink."

❀ First single ....

....

....

❀ Weeks at number one

....

75

TRAVEL TALES

❧ Date .... Time .... Place ....

✿ Have you ever traveled overnight to get somewhere?

Yes ◌ No ◌

If yes, where to? ....

✿ Ever been on a ferry ◌ a cable car ◌ a helicopter ◌

a train ◌ a plane ◌ a boat ◌ a unicycle ◌ ?

✿ Where was the last place you went on vacation?

....

✿ Would you go there again? Yes ◌ No ◌

If no, why not? ....

....

✿ Which destination is the farthest from
home you have ever traveled to?

....

....

ULTIMATE DESTINATION

Date .... Time .... Place ....

Think of four places you'd really love to visit and write one in each space on the first row. Decide which of each pair you would want to visit more, and write them in the spaces on the second row. Now, select the place you would want to visit more than the other: your *ultimate* destination. When you look back at this book, do you think you will have been there?

Are we there yet?

MISS THIS

❧ Date .... Time .... Place .... ❧

Think of ten things you miss when you're away from home. Write your top ten below, with the thing you miss most at number one.

1. ....

2. ....

3. ....

4. ....

5. ....

6. ....

....

7. ....

....

8. ....

....

9. ....

10. ....

DON'T MISS THAT

Date .... Time .... Place ....

Think of ten things that you're glad to get away from when you're away from home. Write your top ten below, with the thing you miss least at number one.

1. ....

....

2. ....

....

3. ....

....

4. ....

5. ....

6. ....

7. ....

8. ....

9. ....

10. ....

FOREVER FOODS

❧ Date .... Time .... Place .... ❧

If you could eat only one item from each list of options below for the rest of your life, which would it be? Check one on each line.

Breakfast. Toast ◯ Cereal ◯ Sausage ◯ Bacon and eggs ◯

Snacks. Chocolate ◯ Cakes ◯ Candy ◯ Pie ◯

Popcorn. Sweet ◯ Salty ◯ Toffee ◯ Plain ◯

Chips. Plain ◯ Ranch ◯ Barbecue ◯ Sour cream and onion ◯

Vegetables. Carrots ◯ Broccoli ◯ Peas ◯ Cauliflower ◯

Carbs. Pasta ◯ Rice ◯ Bread ◯ Potatoes ◯

Ice cream. Chocolate ◯ Strawberry ◯ Vanilla ◯ Mint ◯

Fruit. Oranges ◯ Bananas ◯ Grapes ◯ Apples ◯

Scary. Snails ◯ Frogs' legs ◯ Liver ◯ Fried insects ◯

Memory Box Memento. Glue a wrapper from your favorite candy onto a piece of paper. Write five words around it that describe the sweet (for example, melty, bubbly, chocolatey, yummy, crunchy). Put it in your Memory Box.

ARE YOU A DAREDEVIL?

❧ Date .... Time .... Place .... ❧

Check **A**, **B**, or **C** to answer these daredevil questions, depending on whether you would say, "I'm in!," "maybe" or "no way!" Count up how many of each you have selected, then turn the page to find out how daring you are. So, would you ever . . .

	A I'm in!	B Maybe	C No way!
. . . sky-dive?	○	○	○
. . . swim with sharks?	○	○	○
. . . hold a tarantula?	○	○	○
. . . go upside-down on a carnival ride?	○	○	○
. . . stay in a haunted house?	○	○	○
. . . ride a motorcycle?	○	○	○
. . . bungee jump?	○	○	○
. . . fly a plane?	○	○	○
. . . blast into space?	○	○	○
. . . walk a tightrope?	○	○	○
. . . go whitewater rafting?	○	○	○
. . . dive from the highest board?	○	○	○

DARING ANSWERS

(Mostly **A**s.) **Fearless fanatic.** You are the ultimate daredevil! Always up for a new challenge, you never turn down a dare. You have a fearless attitude and love to take the lead. This sometimes worries people and forces them to put rules in place that stop you from taking things too far.

(Mostly **B**s.) **Balanced babe.** You're a brave lady who's not afraid to try new things, but you always weigh the pros and cons first. You think carefully before taking the plunge, and people give you lots of freedom because they know they can trust you to make the right decision.

(Mostly **C**s.) **Safe sister.** You're a cautious girl who likes to play it safe. You hate being put into risky situations, and are always the first to stop your friends getting into trouble. People respect this, but also encourage you not to be afraid to try new things.

TOP TEN PEOPLE YOU ADMIRE

❧ Date .... Time .... Place .... ❧

Think of ten people that you really admire, then organize them into a top ten list, according to how important they are to you. Your favorite should be number one. Write a name by each number, then say why you admire them on the line underneath.

1. ....
....

2. ....
....

3. ....
....

4. ....
....

5. ....
....

6. ....
....

7. ....
....

8. ....
....

9. ....
....

10. ....
....

Memory Box Memento. Write a letter to the number one person you admire, telling them what you love about them. It doesn't matter whether it's someone you know, someone famous, or even someone who lived long ago. Put a copy of the letter in your Memory Box, and, if possible, send a copy to the person, too. If they write back, put their response in your Memory Box.

YOUR INFLUENCES CLOCK

Date .... Time .... Place ....

Think about the people who've had an impact on you during your life. Perhaps there's a celebrity whose style has influenced your wardrobe, or a friend who's introduced you to a new culture. Write your name or draw a picture of yourself in the center of the clock, then write the names of twelve people who've influenced you around the outside.

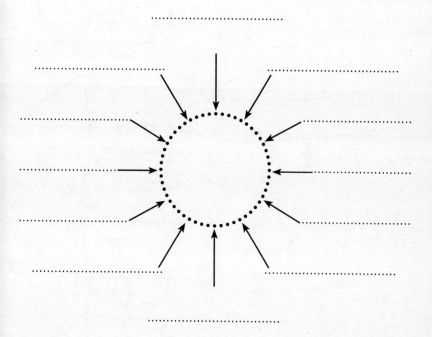

FAMILY FORTUNES

Date .... Time .... Place ....

Ask five family members or close friends to make a wish for you and write it in the fortune cookie papers below. Remember to check back to see if their wishes for you came true.

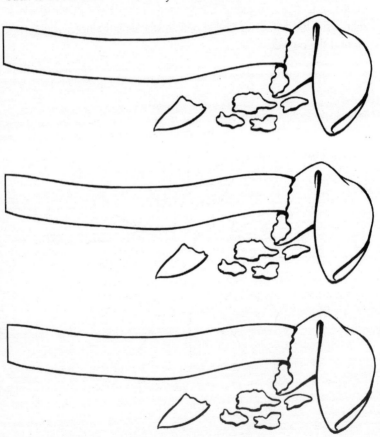

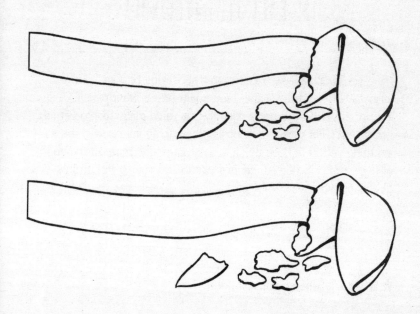

Memory Box Memento. Make a wish for yourself and write it down on a piece of paper. Fold the piece of paper in half and put it inside an envelope. Next, make some wish dust by mixing together as many of the following as you can find: ground cinnamon, ground ginger, cloves, dried flower petals, dried lavender. Sprinkle the dust into the envelope, saying your wish out loud as you do so. Seal the envelope shut and tie a ribbon around it. Put it in your Memory Box and wait for the wish to come true!

IN-DEPTH INTERVIEW

❧ Date .... Time .... Place .... ❧

Have you ever wanted to know more about one of your favorite relatives? This is your chance. You might pick a grandparent, or an aunt or uncle, but choose a relation that you'd really like to get to know better. Put these questions to them in an interview. If there is anything you have been dying to ask, now is the time. At the end of the list of questions, there is space to add your own burning question, to ask your subject.

❀ What is your full name?

....

❀ When and where were you born?

....

❀ Where did you grow up?

....

❀ How are we related?

....

❀ What is your earliest memory?

....

....

❀ What's your earliest memory of me?

....

....

....

❀ What did you want to be when you grew up?

....

....

....

❀ What did you actually do?

....

....

....

❀ What is your proudest achievement?

....

....

....

....

❁ What is the most important news event that has happened in your lifetime?

....

....

....

....

❁ What is your favorite place in the whole world, and why?

....

....

....

❁ What did you like most about school?

....

❁ Who was your best friend when you were my age?

....

❁ Which person did you most admire when you were my age?

....

❁ Why? ....

❀ What is the best present you have ever been given?

....

....

....

❀ If you had one piece of advice to give me, what would it be?

....

....

....

❀ My burning question is: ....

....

❀ The answer is: ....

....

What would your own answers to the same questions be?

Memory Box Memento. Once you've noted down the answers to all these questions, ask someone to take a photograph of you with your chosen interviewee. Make a note of the date of the interview on the back of the picture, put both your names on it, and put it in your Memory Box.

PARTY PLANNER

❧ Date .... Time .... Place .... ❧

Just imagine you're an event organizer who's been given an unlimited budget to put together the world's greatest party.

❀ First, what would your party be celebrating?

....

....

❀ All the best parties have a theme, whether it's the color of outfits people can wear, or a particular theme to dress up for – what would yours be?

....

....

....

❀ If you could ask any band, pop star, or DJ to provide the music, who would it be?

....

....

❀ Would there be any other entertainment? Yes ◯ No ◯

If yes, what would it be? ....

....

....

❀ What kind of food and drink would you choose?

....

....

....

....

❀ What would you wear?

....

....

....

❀ If you could ask anyone in the world to go with you to the party, who would it be?

....

....

PERSONAL PROFILER

❧ Date .... Time .... Place .... ❧

Answer these questions, and make a note of how many times you answer **a**, **b**, **c**, or **d**, then turn to page 96 to discover the secrets of your personality.

❀ What do you love most about your best friend?

    a. You never know what she's going to do next.
    b. She's always first to know when there's a party.
    c. She totally understands you.
    d. You can always rely on her to be there for you.

❀ Your friend calls you in tears. What do you do?

    a. Listen carefully and try to help her see that it's not so bad.
    b. Suggest an activity to take her mind off the problem.
    c. Head straight to her house with a tub of ice cream.
    d. Offer some practical solutions to the problem.

❀ Which do you find most annoying?

    a. Being made to follow lots of rules.
    b. Being grounded.
    c. Being lied to.
    d. Being rushed into a quick decision.

❀ A friend comes over to ask you to the park. What do you do?

    a. Immediately go with her.
    b. Call other people on the way.
    c. Invite her in for a snack and a chat first.
    d. Ask her to wait while you grab a few things you'll need.

❀ During lunch, where can you usually be found?

a. Painting in the art room.
b. Hanging out in a big group.
c. Having an intense chat with your best friend.
d. Flicking through magazines.

❀ What do you prefer to watch on TV?

a. You don't really watch much TV.
b. Music programs.
c. Soap operas with characters you can really relate to.
d. Documentaries about amazing animals and beautiful places.

❀ What's your bedroom like?

a. Full of color.
b. A bit of a mess, with loads of photos of friends on the walls.
c. Peaceful – a tranquil retreat.
d. Everything's in exactly the right place. It's perfectly organized.

❀ Your friend is off to a party and asks you to do her hair. What do you do?

a. Create an amazing new style.
b. Let her choose from all the latest styles in magazines.
c. Do it exactly the way she wants.
d. Use a straightener and lots of products to create a sensational style.

YOUR PERSONAL PROFILE ANSWERS

(Mostly **a**s.) **Bohemian babe.** Unconventional and imaginative, you're a true free spirit. Your spontaneous nature means that life's never dull when you're around. You think with your heart and always follow your instincts. You rarely think about the practicalities of situations, which can sometimes get you into trouble!

(Mostly **b**s.) **Social butterfly.** Warm-hearted and easygoing, you have loads of friends and are always the life and soul of the party. You're super-confident and feel comfortable meeting new people and going into new situations. Don't forget to take some time out to unwind every now and then.

(Mostly **c**s.) **Caring and kind.** A great friend, you're always there for people when they need you. You build strong, deep relationships and prefer to spend time with people you love and trust. You're in touch with your feelings and have strong emotions. Beware of being overly sensitive.

(Mostly **d**s.) **Smart cookie.** A bright spark, you're highly intelligent and a quick thinker. You're practical, logical, and can take care of yourself in any situation. People admire your down-to-earth approach to life. You have lots of interests and know your own mind, but don't be afraid to just go with the flow every now and then.

BEST GAMES OF ALL TIME

❧ Date .... Time .... Place .... ☙

Compile a list of your top-ten favorite games, in order of how much you like them. They might be computer games, playground games, or even games you've invented with your friends. Make sure that your favorite game is listed at number one.

1. ....

2. ....

3. ....

4. ....

5. ....

6. ....

7. ....

8. ....

9. ....

10. ....

FOUR SEASONS IN ONE PAGE

Date .... Time .... Place ....

In the spaces below, use words or pictures to describe the things you like best about each of the seasons. Think about the weather, the kinds of clothes you wear, the activities you do, and any celebrations that take place at that time of year.

Spring

Summer

Fall

Winter

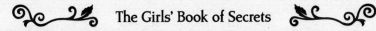

IF I WERE . . .

❧ Date .... Time .... Place .... ❧

What kind of character do you have? Are you energetic and playful? Or perhaps you're quiet and thoughtful? Think about the kind of person you are and the things that you like, then decide what you'd be in each of the categories below. For example, if you are an energetic, playful person, you might choose a Labrador puppy as the animal you'd be.

❀ If I were an animal, I'd be a ....

❀ If I were a drink, I'd be a ....

❀ If I were a color, I'd be ....

❀ If I were a country, I'd be ....

❀ If I were a store, I'd be ....

❀ If I were a pop star, I'd be ....

❀ If I were a musical instrument, I'd be a ....

❀ If I were an ice-cream flavor, I'd be ....

❀ If I were a school subject, I'd be ....

❀ If I were a fairy-tale character, I'd be ....

❀ If I were a sport, I'd be ....

SUPERPOWER SHOWDOWN

Date .... Time .... Place ....

Think of four superpowers that you would most like to have – these could be anything from being invisible to being able to stop time. Write one in each space on the top row. Then choose which superpower from each pair you would more like to have. Write one in each space on the second row. Lastly, decide which of the final two is the *ultimate* superpower you would like to have.

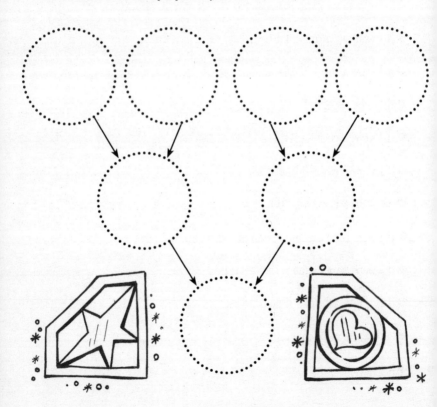

YOUR SUPERHERO COSTUME

The greatest superheroes always have a super-stylish outfit so that they stand out from the crowd. This way, in a difficult situation people know just who to turn to for help. Design a spectacular costume of your own in the space on the right. What would your superhero name be? Fill it in below.

....

GUILTY PLEASURES

❧ Date .... Time .... Place .... ❧

Think of things you know you shouldn't like, yet
you can't help but love. Perhaps there's a cheesy
song that isn't cool but always gets you dancing.
Or maybe a toy that's for little kids you still like
to play with! Write four of these things in the
top row, then choose which from each pair
you enjoy more in the second row. Out of
the final two, you must decide which is your
ultimate guilty pleasure.

BODY TRICKS

Date .... Time .... Place ....

Check off each thing that you and your friends can do.

Fill out each person's name in the spaces along the top.

Roll your tongue into a tube	○	○	○	○	○	○
Wiggle your ears	○	○	○	○	○	○
Raise one eyebrow	○	○	○	○	○	○
Touch your nose with your tongue	○	○	○	○	○	○
Lick your elbow	○	○	○	○	○	○
Twitch your nose	○	○	○	○	○	○

Is there anything else you can do that none of your friends can?

Yes ○ No ○

If yes, describe what it is here:

....

....

....

FINGERPRINT FUN

Date .... Time .... Place ....

TAKE YOUR PRINTS

Draw around your hand on the page opposite. Then dip the top of each of your fingers in some paint, or an ink pad if you have one. Carefully press each fingertip onto the corresponding finger on the page to record your fingerprints. Why not get each of your friends to do the same on a separate piece of paper and compare prints?

DID YOU KNOW?

❀ Most people say that each human fingerprint is unique, but this isn't necessarily true. The only way you'd know for certain is to check the fingerprints of everyone who has ever lived! In fact, different people's fingerprints can sometimes be similar enough even to fool experts, leading to several cases of mistaken identity.

❀ Your fingernails (and toenails, for that matter) are made from the same stuff as your hair – keratin. This is a protein that is also found in birds' feathers and animals' hooves.

❀ The nails on your fingers grow faster than those on your toes, with the nail on your middle finger usually growing fastest.

❀ Fingernails do not continue to grow after you die, as some people claim. It is the skin around the nails shrinking back that makes them appear longer.

❀ If you stopped moving your hand for a long enough time, the lines on your palms and fingers would eventually smooth out.

Draw around your hand here.

Why not doodle some patterns on your hand once you've finished your fingerprints?

HOW'S YOUR HOLISTIC HEALTH?

❧ Date .... Time .... Place .... ❧

Holistic comes from a Greek word that means "whole." Holistic health looks at all areas of your life and how they affect your well-being. On the diagram below, give a rating out of ten for each question, according to how you rate the quality of each part of your life. Zero is center of the circle, ten is the outside edge. Join the points you've marked to see what shape they make. The closer they are to a perfect circle (the larger, the better), the better your holistic health.

How good is your family life?

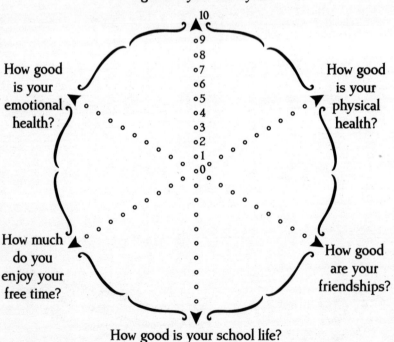

How good is your emotional health?

How good is your physical health?

How much do you enjoy your free time?

How good are your friendships?

How good is your school life?

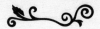

WHAT A WEEK!

Experts recommend that you should eat at least five portions of fruit and vegetables every day, and do at least 30 minutes' of exercise. You should also get eight hours of sleep every night, but it's important to spend some quality time relaxing, too. Stress is bad for the body and your mind, and laughter is said to be the best medicine. So the more time you spend laughing, the better it is for your health.

Over a week, keep a record of the following:

	Hours of sleep	Pieces of fruit	Portions of veggies	Minutes of exercise	Minutes relaxing	Minutes laughing
Monday	☐	☐	☐	☐	☐	☐
Tuesday	☐	☐	☐	☐	☐	☐
Wednesday	☐	☐	☐	☐	☐	☐
Thursday	☐	☐	☐	☐	☐	☐
Friday	☐	☐	☐	☐	☐	☐
Saturday	☐	☐	☐	☐	☐	☐
Sunday	☐	☐	☐	☐	☐	☐

How did you do over seven days? Great ◯ Okay ◯ Badly ◯

Any areas where you could make improvements? Yes ◯ No ◯

If yes, which ones? ....

ULTIMATE CONFESSIONS

❧ Date .... Time .... Place .... ❧

It's time to confess your ultimate secrets! But don't worry, no one will be able to find out what they are. Here's how to create a tamper-proof file to put in your Memory Box.

1. Find a large envelope and write "Homework" on it in black marker – this will put off any snoops looking for gossip!

2. Find some pretty notepaper and envelopes. Write one secret per page and seal each secret in a separate envelope.

Your secrets might include:

> The most embarrassing thing that's ever happened to you, so far.

> The name of the boy you like.

> Something you did wrong that someone else got the blame for.

> Something you'd like to say to someone, but don't dare.

3. Place all the envelopes inside the larger envelope. Seal the envelope shut. You could also place stickers over the seal so that you'll know for certain if someone has taken a peek.

4. Place your "Homework" at the bottom of your Memory Box and pile everything else you have collected on top.

BEST FRIENDS FOREVER?

Date .... Time .... Place ....

How well do you and your friends know each other? Read through the questions below and fill in your own answers. (Copy out the questions for your friends to fill in, too.) Then quiz your friends to find out just how well they know you. Make a note of the number of questions they each get right. Turn the page for the results.

1. What date is my birthday?

....

2. What is my favorite color?

....

3. Who is my celebrity crush?

....

4. What is my favorite animal?

....

5. What is my favorite food?

....

6. What do I want to be when I grow up?

....

7. What is my most embarrassing moment, so far?

....

8. What is my all-time favorite movie?

....

9. What is my all-time favorite book?

....

10. Where in the world would I most like to visit?

....

11. What would my ideal Saturday be?

....

12. Which three words would I use to describe myself?

....

THE SCORES

1–4. Oops! Looks like you need to spend a little more quality time together and get to know each other better.

5–8. You are certainly good friends, but you've still got some sharing to do before you become true best buds.

9–12. Wow. You're as close as sisters and have no secrets from each other – you can always rely on one another in a crisis.

ADVICE CHALLENGE

🌿 Date .... Time .... Place .... 🌿

Advice columnists often work for newspapers and magazines. They help with problems that readers send in by offering their advice. Why not get together with a group of friends and choose a problem to respond to? Discuss the advice you could give if someone asked your opinion. Practice your own skills by providing an answer to one of the following problems. You can also fill in your name in the spaces provided.

Dear ....

A new girl has started at my school and my best friend has been spending tons of time with her. I'm feeling really left out and keep arguing with my best friend. What should I do?

Dear ....

My sister is so annoying! She is a massive show-off and gets all the attention. She is younger than me and whenever she does something wrong I get the blame. Help!

Dear ....
I'm finding it difficult to fit in everything I want to do at the moment. We're getting tons of homework and I belong to lots of after-school clubs. I don't want to give them up, but my grades are bad. Do you have any ideas?'

Dear ....
I feel like I'm always being compared to my older sister. She's really smart and always gets good grades at school. She's also popular and has lots of friends. How can I deal with the pressure to do as well as her?'

WHAT'S YOUR PROBLEM?

With your friends, think of three problems you would like to ask an expert about. Put them in order, with the most important problem at number one. See if you and your friends can come up with any solutions yourselves, or ask a parent for advice.

1. ....

....

2. ....

....

3. ....

....

PET PROFILE

Date ....

Time .... Place ....

Complete the information below, either about your favorite pet or a dream pet that you'd love to own.

Name .... Age ....

Type of animal ....

Boy ◯ Girl ◯ Color ....

Likes ....

Dislikes ....

What's the funniest thing your pet does?

....

What's the naughtiest thing your pet does?

....

A FEW OF MY FAVORITE THINGS

❧ Date .... Time .... Place .... ❧

Imagine you are marooned on a desert island. Which items from your personal belongings would you be lost without? You would already have all necessary practical items, so these should be things that you love and would enjoy while waiting to be rescued. Organize your list into a top ten, according to how bored or sad you'd be without them. Your favorite should be at number one.

1. ....

2. ....

3. ....

4. ....

5. ....

6. ....

7. ....

8. ....

9. ....

10. ....

SURVIVAL SKILLS

❧ Date .... Time .... Place .... ❧

If you were marooned on a desert island, but without any essential items, which of the following challenges would you be willing to attempt while waiting to be rescued? Turn to page 116 to find out your skill rating.

	A Absolutely	B Maybe	C No way!
Build a fire	○	○	○
Read a map	○	○	○
Catch a fish	○	○	○
Dig a well	○	○	○
Make a raft	○	○	○
Build a shelter	○	○	○
Make an animal trap	○	○	○
Escape from quicksand	○	○	○
Make a bow and arrow	○	○	○
Use leaves as toilet paper	○	○	○
Eat bugs	○	○	○

SURVIVAL ANSWERS

(Mostly **A**s.) **Super survivor.** Your survival skills are top notch and you love the great outdoors. You feel as at home in a forest as most people would in a five-star hotel! If necessary, you could take care of yourself for weeks on end, but with your excellent navigation skills you'd probably find your way to that hotel in no time at all.

(Mostly **B**s.) **Adventurous amiga.** You haven't had the opportunity to practice many survival skills, but you're an adventurous girl who would love to give it a try! You don't mind getting your hands dirty (or eating the odd bug for survival). Why not persuade your parents to take you on a camping trip?

(Mostly **C**s.) **Indoor individual.** Outdoor living is not for you, and you wouldn't last long if you were stranded on your own. You're accustomed to the finer things in life and wouldn't even like to stay on a campsite equipped with showers and a restaurant!

WOULD YOU RATHER?

❧ Date .... Time .... Place .... ☙

Study each option below and decide which you would rather choose if you really had to – there is no "neither" option!

✿ Have no eyebrows ⭘

Have eyebrows that meet in the middle ⭘

✿ Never wash your hair again ⭘

Never wash your pants again ⭘

✿ Be popular but ugly ⭘ Be beautiful but unpopular ⭘

✿ Have no TV ⭘ Have a TV that only showed commercials ⭘

✿ Never listen to any music again ⭘

Always listen to classical music ⭘

✿ Spend a night in a haunted house ⭘

Spend a night on your own in the woods ⭘

❀ Have hiccups for a month ⦂

Do nothing but math for a whole day ⦂

❀ Be able to paint your nails just by looking at them ⦂

Be able to style your hair just by thinking about it ⦂

❀ Burp every time a boy talks to you ⦂

Fart every time a girl talks to you ⦂

❀ Go to school in just your underwear for a day ⦂

Go to school in a clown outfit for one month ⦂

❀ Never read a magazine again ⦂

Never go to the movies again ⦂

❀ Find a secret treasure ⦂

Make a new friend ⦂

BEST MOMENTS OF ALL TIME

Date .... Time .... Place ....

Think of the best things that have ever happened to you (so far) –
perhaps when a baby brother or sister was born, or the feeling you
got the first time you rode a bike without help. Perhaps you won an
award that you're really proud of, or you held your first sleepover
and it was a huge success. Once you've thought of your five best
moments, list them in order so that your all-time favorite is at
number one.

1. ....

....

2. ....

....

3. ....

....

4. ....

....

5. ....

....

HEADLINE NEWS

❧ Date .... Time .... Place .... ❧

Have you noticed what's going on in the news lately? What do you think are the five most important news stories at the moment? Make a list and write them in order so that the one that you think is most memorable is at number one.

1. ....

2. ....

3. ....

4. ....

5. ....

HEADLINE-MAKER

❧ Date .... Time .... Place .... ❧

What are the five most important things that happened to you this week? Make a list of these events, so that the most important event is at number one.

1. ....

2. ....

3. ....

4. ....

5. ....

SIGN OF THE TIMES

Ask each of your best friends to sign their name in the space below for you to look back at in the future.

SOCIAL BUTTERFLY OR BUTTERFLIES IN YOUR TUMMY?

Date .... Time .... Place ....

Study each option below and decide which you would choose each time.

❀ Karaoke queen ◌ Backup singer ◌

❀ Actress ◌ Stage manager ◌

❀ All night party ◌ Pajama party ◌

❀ Leader of the pack ◌ Team player ◌

❀ Vintage dress ◌ Trendy T-shirt ◌

❀ Night owl ◌ Early bird ◌

❀ Bikini ◌ One-piece ◌

❀ The camera loves me ◌ Camera shy ◌

❀ Busy, busy, busy ◌ Me time ◌

❀ Partygoer ◌ Party planner ◌

❀ New faces ◌ Old friends ◌

❀ First on the dance floor ◌ Two left feet ◌

❀ Giving speeches ◌ Writing speeches ◌

❀ Fashionably late ◌ Right on time ◌

FRIENDSHIP GALLERY

❧ Date .... Time .... Place .... ❧

Get four friends to each draw a portrait of you in one of these frames. Each friend should write a caption describing you underneath their artwork and sign their work when they are finished.

....

....

....

Signed .... **Signed** ....

....

....

....

Signed ....   Signed ....

Memory Box Memento. Get someone to take a photograph of you and your friends together, print it, and write each of your names and the date on the back. Place it in your Memory Box to look back at in years to come.

THE MOVIE OF YOUR LIFE . . .

Date .... Time .... Place ....

You're such an incredible girl that someone is sure to want to make a movie about your life one day. Obviously you'll get the final casting choice, so who would you choose to play you, your family, and your friends? Write the name of each character you would want in the movie in the column on the left, then which actor you think should play the part in the column on the right.

Role	Played by
....	....
....	....
....	....
....	....
....	....
....	....
....	....
....	....
....	....

BEST MOVIES OF ALL TIME

❧ Date .... Time .... Place .... ❧

Can you decide which are the ten best movies you have ever seen?
Once you've decided what they are, organize your list into a top ten,
according to how much you enjoy them, with the very best movie at
number one.

1. ....

2. ....

3. ....

4. ....

5. ....

6. ....

7. ....

8. ....

9. ....

10. ....

ALSO AVAILABLE ...

The Boys' Book: How To Be
The Best At Everything
978-0-545-01628-5

The Girls' Book: How To Be
The Best At Everything
978-0-545-01629-2

Thirty Days Has September:
Cool Ways To Remember
Stuff
978-0-545-10740-2

The Boys' Book of Survival:
How To Survive Anything,
Anywhere
978-0-545-08536-6

The Girls' Book of
Glamour: A Guide To
Being A Goddess
978-0-545-08537-3

Practices that Improve
Teaching Evaluation

Grace French-Lazovik, *Editor*

NEW DIRECTIONS FOR TEACHING AND LEARNING
KENNETH E. EBLE and JOHN F. NOONAN, *Editors-in-Chief*

Number 11, September 1982

Paperback sourcebooks in
The Jossey-Bass Higher Education Series

Jossey-Bass Inc., Publishers
San Francisco • Washington • London

Practices that Improve Teaching Evaluation
Number 11, September 1982
  Grace French-Lazovik, *Editor*

New Directions for Teaching and Learning Series
Kenneth E. Eble and John F. Noonan, *Editors-in-Chief*

New Directions for Teaching and Learning is published quarterly
by Jossey-Bass Inc., Publishers. Subscriptions, single-issue
orders, change of address notices, undelivered copies, and other
correspondence should be sent to *New Directions* Subscriptions,
Jossey-Bass Inc., Publishers, 433 California Street, San Francisco,
California 94104.

Editorial correspondence should be sent to the Editors-in-Chief,
Kenneth E. Eble or John F. Noonan, Center for Improving
Teaching Effectiveness, Virginia Commonwealth University,
Richmond, Virginia 23284.

Library of Congress Catalogue Card Number LC 81-48584
International Standard Serial Number ISSN 0271-0633
International Standard Book Number ISBN 87589-925-0

Cover art by Willi Baum
Manufactured in the United States of America

Ordering Information

The paperback sourcebooks listed below are published quarterly and can be ordered either by subscription or as single copies.

Subscriptions cost $35.00 per year for institutions, agencies, and libraries. Individuals can subscribe at the special rate of $21.00 per year *if payment is by personal check.* (Note that the full rate of $35.00 applies if payment is by institutional check, even if the subscription is designated for an individual.) Standing orders are accepted.

Single copies are available at $7.95 when payment accompanies order, and *all single-copy orders under $25.00 must include payment.* (California, Washington, D.C., New Jersey, and New York residents please include appropriate sales tax.) For billed orders, cost per copy is $7.95 plus postage and handling. (Prices subject to change without notice.)

To ensure correct and prompt delivery, all orders must give either the *name of an individual* or an *official purchase order number.* Please submit your order as follows:

Subscriptions: specify series and subscription year.
Single Copies: specify sourcebook code and issue number (such as, TL8).

Mail orders for United States and Possessions, Latin America, Canada, Japan, Australia, and New Zealand to:
Jossey-Bass Inc., Publishers
433 California Street
San Francisco, California 94104

Mail orders for all other parts of the world to:
Jossey-Bass Limited
28 Banner Street
London EC1Y 8QE

New Directions for Teaching and Learning Series
Kenneth E. Eble and John F. Noonan, *Editors-in-Chief*

Contents

of due process threaten higher education's independence, and what simple steps can diminish this threat?

Editor's Notes

My early thoughts about what should go into this volume focused on summarizing the research literature on teaching evaluation. This literature has mushroomed in recent decades, is scattered in many places, and is not easily accessible, except to the specialist. Before my efforts could begin, however, this goal to summarize was eminently accomplished by the appearance of books by John Centra (1979) and Peter Seldin (1980) and by Wilbert McKeachie's excellent summary article in *Academe* (1979), "Student Ratings of Faculty: A Reprise." Clearly, another summary of the research literature was not needed.

There is, however, a considerable body of expertise that has not been tapped in most writings, for it arises not out of research, though it makes abundant use of research findings, but out of experience—the experience of being long engaged in serious efforts to foster sound evaluation of teaching practices. From such experience comes knowledge of the best ways to achieve evaluation systems that contribute to excellence but, at the same time, preserve policies of openness and fairness. Advice from those who have learned to negotiate the tortuous path to a good evaluation system can provide insights very hard to come by in any other way—advice that may help to make that path easier for others to follow.

All of the authors of these chapters have had long experience with the problems of evaluating college teaching, though at different types of academic institutions; all have written and lectured about these problems; and all share the perspective of having been both faculty member and administrator, though their administrative roles have differed widely, as do some of their views. There is, however, a remarkable consensus among these authors on the crucial issues that all must face.

The principal focus of the advice offered here concerns the roles and responsibilities of those involved in the evaluative process: administrators, department chairpersons, evaluation directors, and faculty peer committees. A second theme emphasizes policies that encourage faculty trust in the evaluation procedures and that provide due process in academic decisions. The final chapter summarizes some of the benchmarks that should be present if a teaching evaluation system is to be used summatively.

Grace French-Lazovik
Editor

1

2

References

Centra, J. A. *Determining Faculty Effectiveness.* San Francisco: Jossey-Bass, 1979.
McKeachie, W. J. "Student Ratings of Faculty: A Reprise." *Academe,* 1979, *65,* 384–397.
Seldin, P. *Successful Faculty Evaluation Programs.* Crugers, N.Y.: Coventry, 1980.

Grace French-Lazovik is director of the Office for the Evaluation of Teaching at the University of Pittsburgh. Her work in teaching evaluation began over thirty years ago at the University of Washington with Professor Edwin Guthrie, one of the field's earliest pioneers.

*Efforts to change the evaluation of teaching must be
part of a process to improve all aspects of faculty
evaluation. These efforts will not succeed without
effective leadership by academic administrators,
which has been found to be essential for successful
revision of evaluation practices.*

The Role of Administrators
in Changing Teaching
Evaluation Procedures

William R. O'Connell, Jr.
Jon F. Wergin

Evaluation has always been a fundamental element in the educational
process. Students have always been evaluated at periodic intervals; before
faculty members are recruited, each candidate's background and capabilities are assessed; and all colleges and universities evaluate their faculty—
formally or informally, tacitly or openly—for salary, promotion, and
tenure decisions, and to identify characteristics in need of improvement.
In spite of this tradition of evaluating, faculty evaluation continues to be
troublesome, and at some institutions it has been the source of problems
that affect morale and personal growth. There have also been instances
where it has led to legal action.

Declining student enrollments, decreased faculty mobility, and
increased financial pressures on colleges and universities create a critical
need for more attention to affirmative action, specific and concrete expla-
nations for decisions that are made, and fair and equitable policies on
promotion and tenure. At the same time, the legal ramifications of some
of these activities make them increasingly complex. There has also been a

G. French-Lazovik (Ed.). *New Directions for Teaching and Learning:*
Practices that Improve Teaching Evaluation, no. 11. San Francisco: Jossey-Bass, September 1982.

growing concern on the part of many administrators and faculty members about the need to improve instruction.

All of these conditions have intensified the desire of both faculty and administrators to achieve equity in making decisions about faculty members, and this desire has, in large part, stimulated the increased concern about faculty evaluation in American colleges and universities since the mid-1970s. A great deal of attention has been given to examining the approaches and procedures used for evaluating faculty in their various roles, particularly in the teaching function itself.

The interest in improving faculty evaluation procedures continues to be high, judging from attendance at regional and national conferences and workshops, the frequent appearance of articles and other publications on the subject, the presentations of various professional and academic meetings, and the variety of evaluation-related projects undertaken in recent years. While many of the concerns about faculty evaluation are common across an institution, *the impetus for change most often comes from administrators,* since they are responsible for institutional operations and the legal ramifications of evaluation. Administrators are also aware of the need for responsiveness to students' concerns about the quality of education they receive. Finally, administrators must respond to increasing pressure from legislators, trustees, and the community in general to account for the work taking place in the institution and to demonstrate quality performance.

This chapter presents a number of institutional conditions that support the need for improved faculty evaluation policies, and it suggests specific strategies that administrators can use to implement improvements in the evaluation process.

The Need to Evaluate Teaching Within the Context of Overall Faculty Evaluation

Although the focus of this chapter is on the evaluation of instruction, it is important to note that any attempt to change teaching evaluation policies should also examine policies on all aspects of a faculty member's performance, including research, clinical practice, and service. In fact, the evidence suggests that new teaching evaluation policies and procedures will not succeed unless they are incorporated into a larger faculty evaluation package.

In the past few years, the emphasis in the literature on this subject has been on the evaluation of teaching. There is no doubt that teaching effectiveness is not easily defined and measured in standard, quantifiable terms, and that improvements are needed in the evaluation process. Standards and criteria are sometimes both obscure and highly variable, particularly from one discipline to another. Administrators are thus often left with enormous interpretation problems. However, if the evaluation of teaching is considered within the context of an overall faculty evaluation system, then interdepartment disparities can be examined as they affect other areas of academic responsibility as well.

One compelling reason for considering teaching along with other academic duties is that the entire range of a faculty member's responsibilities should be weighted in relation to the institution's values and priorities. In a research-oriented setting, for example, where faculty members spend considerable time writing grant proposals and conducting research projects, and proportionately less time in the classroom, the amount of weight given to teaching evaluations should be less. In a liberal arts college, on the other hand, more weight should be placed on such evaluations, since the college itself places a greater emphasis on teaching.

This weighting process is complicated, however, by the fact that the distinctions among various faculty responsibilities are often blurred. For instance, is the coordination of continuing education programs a teaching activity, a service activity, or an administrative activity? In order to avoid artificial or inconsistent distinctions, therefore, administrators must consider the institution's mission as they attempt to change evaluation policies.

Another reason that teaching evaluation should be examined in the context of overall evaluation is that there are many unresolved questions concerning the computerized rating systems that many institutions have instituted in recent years. There is no clear consensus on how such data relate to information not only on other aspects of teaching, such as course development, but also on nonteaching functions. How much influence should such data carry, and what criteria should govern such determinations? To what extent are any noted deficiencies in one area compensated for by outstanding achievements in another? These are difficult questions, but they must be considered seriously if an administrator is to avoid the temptation of using only computer-generated reports for faculty evaluation.

Yet another consideration is the potential for application of standards. Clearly, both the type and extent of teaching responsibilities vary considerably from one faculty member to another. Focusing strictly on teaching effectiveness in the broadest sense, therefore, is bound to affect faculty members in disparate ways. Since new systems tend to generate more data than were available previously, there is likely to be more detailed and extensive data available for evaluation of the faculty member with the heavier teaching load.

Attempts to change teaching evaluation policies and procedures without examining the entire faculty reward system also have a "spotlight" effect; that is, a faculty member could think that teaching effectiveness is being singled out to help the administration justify negative decisions, rather than to back up a stated commitment to reward good teaching. "The name of the game around here is still the number of publications you have, and all of these teaching ratings won't help me a bit; but they will be used if someone wants to deny me tenure." Such grievances may be alleviated if an earnest attempt is made to scrutinize the entire faculty evaluation package.

The Need for Change in Evaluation Procedures

At any given time, a significant number of the nation's colleges and universities are in the process of assessing or revising overall institutional procedures, including those for faculty evaluation. Such periodic assessment is generally undertaken because the procedures become ineffective or because there is a general dissatisfaction with them. Occasionally, as support for an existing program wanes, there is a desire to make changes simply for the sake of change. Since it is inherently difficult to devise uniform and objective mechanisms for measuirng human performance, such reassessment is to be expected. The following subsections look at the concerns of administrators and faculty that motivate the reassessment of faculty evaluation.

Concerns of Administrators. Many administrators believe the data available for faculty evaluation are so diverse, and in many cases so fragmented, that they are unreliable and therefore cannot, or should not, be used. In particular, data for the evaluation of teaching often seem even less concrete than those used in the overall faculty evaluation process.

Another administrative concern is that evaluation data frequently are not comparable across an institution, especially in large, multidepartmental institutions that have a wide range of faculty groupings with vastly different roles and responsibilities. Also, the data for *individual* faculty members frequently are not comparable because of differences in individual assignments and responsibilities or differences in the way the data are presented.

Institutions today are under increasing outside pressure to demonstrate quality performance and to provide evidence that they are accomplishing the goals and purposes for which they have been established. These institutions must support teaching excellence in more tangible ways than in the past, especially if their major emphasis is on teaching. This new accountability emphasizes the need for a reassessment of the evaluation procedures now in use.

Finally, administrators are concerned about appropriate affirmative action, about avoiding legal charges brought by faculty who are denied positive recommendations or tenure, and about eliminating competition or conflict between faculty members, different programs, or different colleges within the institution. All of these concerns also reinforce the need to establish equitable, consistent policies of evaluation.

Faculty Concerns. The most pervasive concerns of faculty members seem to be for equity in the decision-making process to ensure fair and comprehensive evaluations and for a uniform policy toward evaluation across the institution.

Another faculty concern is for consistency between policy and practice. Many institutions make public statements about the priority they place on the teaching function, yet they often base rewards on criteria that are unrelated to teaching. Moreover, although many institutions contend that evaluations are based on the faculty member's teaching ability, the information collected often does not help determine this ability.

Additionally, faculty members wish to receive regular feedback on teaching performance early in their careers. The traditional practice of evaluating faculty only at the time for a tenure decision is no longer appropriate. It is much more useful and productive for an institution to provide early evaluation of faculty members' ability, so they are aware of their progress and of what they can do to improve their chances of permanent acceptance into the college or university.

The Conditions Necessary for Making Changes

For many reasons, faculty members typically are not enthusiastic about faculty evaluation. Evaluation, after all, attempts the difficult task of analyzing complex and subjective matters in a simple and ostensibly objective fashion. Participation either as the evaluator or as the one being evaluated diverts time and energies from more central activities and faculty responsibilities. Especially frustrating are efforts to develop new or revised approaches to faculty evaluation, given the general resistance to change and innovation in higher education. However, good faculty evaluation procedures cannot be legislated, and considerable care must be taken if desired changes are to be developed and implemented successfully.

By observing thirty colleges and universities in the process of changing their faculty evaluation systems between 1977 and 1979, we identified a number of conditions that can enhance efforts to bring about improvements. These thirty institutions were part of a regional project conducted by the Southern Regional Education Board (SREB) and funded by the Fund for the Improvement of Postsecondary Education. A brief summary of the process is provided here, since the results achieved by the participating institutions were greatly affected by the extent of administrative involvement on each campus. A full report of this project has been published by SREB (O'Connell and Smartt, 1979).

The thirty institutions participated, through four-member campus teams of faculty and administrators, in a series of regional workshops aimed at planning new or revised faculty evaluation programs. As a follow-up to each workshop, consultants worked with the campus teams on specific local concerns. Each institution determined its own objectives for the project: fifteen sought to design a completely new program; nine focused on part of a larger system, such as working on students' ratings; and six teams set out to review their existing programs and make policies and procedures more consistent within their institutions.

The project evaluators found evidence of significant progress toward these objectives in twenty-six of the thirty schools. In addition, ten schools showed excellent prospects that their innovations would have long-term impact, and fifteen others showed good promise of sustained impact. In short, the project was judged successful.

The project included an analysis of the factors that seemed to distinguish the more successful from the less successful of the thirty institutions. The institutions were divided into three groups: high probability for success, medium probability for success, and low probability for success. The results of this analysis are revealing, particularly as they relate to administrative roles.

Major Factors Responsible for Success. In assessing the project results, the evaluators looked for characteristics that seemed to differentiate the most successful from the least successful projects. When a characteristic common to the "high-probability" institutions was identified, "medium" and "low" institutions were then examined for the absence of that characteristic.

Active Administrative Support. One of the most pervasive factors revealed by the analysis was the active support and involvement of top-level administrators. At all of the institutions in the "high-probability" group, the president or academic vice-president voiced support early in the project, strongly communicated a sense of the need for change, and actively participated in the development of the new system. Conversely, all institutions characterized by a seemingly indifferent administration fell into the "low-probability" group. The apparent influence of this factor was so pronounced that even the *amount* of administrative support correlated almost perfectly with the degree of project success.

Such support took many forms, ranging from strong presidential directives backed up by resolutions from the board of trustees, to the presence of "line" administrators as active and working members of the team. At one college, for example, the president took every opportunity at faculty meetings to voice his full support for a new faculty evaluation system. At another institution, the academic dean worked behind the scenes to obtain three years of grant support for administrative staff and faculty to explore fully new evaluation procedures.

The negative consequences of a lack of top administrative involvement are illustrated by examining one of the "low-probability" schools. Here, team members conscientiously and enthusiastically participated in the project; they drew upon SREB resources, enlisted the aid of consultants, and kept the rest of the faculty well informed of, and involved in, their activities. But their project was given only minimal administrative support, and this created an almost insurmountable barrier. Clearly, therefore, the importance of both strong and active administrative support cannot be overestimated.

Much of the literature on organizational change cites administrative involvement as a key variable. Mayhew (1976) goes so far as to say, "The evidence from the cases studied suggests that strong administrative support by the executive hierarchy of the college or university is the most important condition necessary for innovation and change in higher education" (p. 9). Watson (1961) lists "administrative support" as one of his well-known principles for overcoming resistance to change. Conrad (1978), who studied curriculum change in depth at four institutions, found that the most successful administrators became *agents* rather than *advocates* of change—that is, they seemed both to provide the impetus for change and to negotiate compromises. Maguire (1977), in his discussion of "institutionalizing" change, notes that one of the "required conditions" for successful innovation is the willingness of top administrators to achieve a "ripple effect" and to make political trade-offs.

It was the combination of personal interest and active involvement, coupled with formal authority, that made administrative support such a powerful factor in improving faculty evaluation programs in the thirty institutions studied. Mere administrative proclamations of support without attendant involvement simply did not work. Miller's (1974) first guideline for establishing viable mechanisms for faculty evaluation is to "gain support at the top." The evidence collected both in the SREB project and elsewhere certainly supports that point.

Continued Faculty Involvement. Faculty involvement throughout the project was another characteristic of all the "high-probability" institutions. Each of these institutions expanded the campus team at least temporarily, to include wider faculty representation. Open meetings or workshops were held periodically to keep faculty informed, and team members themselves took the responsibility of keeping their colleagues up-to-date. In addition, feedback from faculty members was solicited and responded to, both formally and informally.

On the other hand, several institutions that had potentially solid plans were included in the "medium-probability" group because the level of faculty involvement was insufficient to generate confidence that the plans would have a lasting impact. Faculty involvement was thus considered another important determining factor in the degree of project success.

The need to involve faculty members who will be most affected by any proposed policy change is almost axiomatic. It heads the list of Watson's (1961) classic features of successful change: the more an innovation is "owned" by those affected by it, the greater will be its full acceptance. Berman and Pauley (1975) reported the results of a Rand Corporation study of innovations in public school settings, and they found that the most successful innovations were those that required the user to work out specific adaptations befitting local needs. The only way this could be done, the authors noted, was to build in procedures for participant involvement in *both* the design and implementation phases of the innovation.

Two of Havelock's (Havelock and others, 1970) well-known factors for successful change are "reward" and "proximity." The former refers to the use of processes that have "pay-off value" to all the parties involved; the latter refers to the opportunity for "meaningful contact and mutual stimulation" between the innovator and other members of the organization. These principles imply that faculty involvement, in order to be meaningful, must be more than an empty co-optation of the interested parties; rather, faculty members must sense their impact on the evolving policies and procedures. Miller (1974) notes that not only must faculty be involved in any effort of this nature but also *key* faculty must be involved (that is, those representing centers of power and influence). He suggests that the lack of involvement of these people early on is one of the most common reasons for failure of faculty evaluation programs.

Miller's point is supported by our own experience in the SREB project. Faculty involvement was built into the project at the start with the formation of representative task forces. In some institutions, however, the task force members made little effort to communicate with their colleagues, and in others the members were not well known on campus. Invariably, these were institutions where little progress was made.

Faculty Trust. The faculty members' trust in the administration was also noted in the "high-probability" institutions. In other words, changes in faculty evaluation procedures were much more likely to be received positively by faculty members when the administration was viewed as responsive to their interests, when administrators took an active listening role, and when faculty concerns were incorporated into evolving plans. In the Rand study cited earlier, Berman and Pauley (1975) found that project outcomes depended more on the characteristics of the project's setting (specifically, on high morale and a sense of shared trust and respect) than on any other single variable. In contrast to other factors that are primarily situation-specific, this element of trust reflects a more general state of organizational health, characterized as "openness" (Havelock and others, 1970), "mutually shared acceptance, trust, and confidence" (Watson, 1961), and "administration and faculty existing in creative tension" (Mayhew, 1976).

Interestingly, our own analysis did not reveal any discernible relationships between the level of faculty trust in administration and the management or decision-making style employed by the top administrator; presidents or academic deans who were generally regarded as "authoritarian" seemed no less likely to be trusted than those who were viewed as "democratic." Administrative effectiveness apparently stems less from the *type* of style employed than from the *consistency* with which the chosen style is used. Therefore, we might conclude that a sizable component of "faculty trust in administration" would depend on the extent to which the administrator supports a project in a manner consistent with his or her behavior in other similar situations. New behaviors may well arouse faculty distrust.

Faculty's Desire for Changes. Faculty dissatisfaction with the status quo did not appear to be critical to the success of the project, but it seems to give institutions having such a characteristic a useful push forward. Faculty dissatisfaction with previous evaluation procedures—due primarily to perceived invalidity or unfairness—helped ward off apathy and the usual organizational resistance to change. This factor was most significant in those institutions attempting to "fine-tune" an intact system; in contrast, satisfaction with the status quo was often a barrier in institutions attempting to develop a new program.

Mayhew (1976) defines this dissatisfaction as "a generally perceived discrepancy between expectation and performance." Most organization theorists would agree that meaningful change is almost impossible without this sense of dissonance. Maguire (1977), for example, lists as one of the most basic obstacles to change "a resistance to thinking about change at all." Conrad (1978) suggests that conflict is an essential prerequisite for change—and that such conflicts are visible only when internal or external pressures threaten the status quo. Another perspective is provided in the Rand study (Berman and Pauley, 1975), which classified each adopting organization studied as "opportunistic" or "problem solving." Opportunistic organizations tended to adopt innovations on the basis of available resources; problem-solving organizations adopted innovations as a response to an identified problem or need. As might be expected, innovations attempted in problem-solving organizations were much more likely to survive.

Historical Acceptance of Faculty Evaluation. This was a characteristic seen more often in smaller institutions without rigid academic and faculty traditions. They generally had greater success in establishing comprehensive evaluation procedures; they usually did not have to deal with the "why evaluate?" question, since expectations of future evaluation are clearly understood at the time of a faculty member's appointment. An atmosphere of openness and trust in organizational change was thus easier to cultivate.

This is another characteristic commonly cited by classical change theorists. Watson (1961) talks of the importance of "compatibility with institutional values," for example. More recently, Mayhew (1976) found consistency with "an institution's history and tradition" to be an important element of successful innovation. What is suggested, perhaps, is that the response to the "creative tension" and "dissatisfaction with the status quo" should be moderate and incremental, not radically different from the way the institution is accustomed to doing things.

An Established Attitude Toward Evaluation. The existence of an institutional statement covering the philosophy and uses of evaluation was a significant factor in the "high-probability" institutions. Many of the projects with serious problems were not operating under a clear sense of purpose for an evaluation system. In other cases, the formulation of such a policy statement appeared to be an event critical to significant progress. At one institution, for example, clear progress was possible only when procedures for evaluation for purposes of improvement were sharply separated from procedures covering promotion and tenure. At another, the implementation of a proposed new formative system was delayed by pressures to use the system for summative purposes.

This factor is closest to Watson's (1961) principle stating the need for clear goals as a prerequisite for innovation and to the "structure" factor (Havelock and others, 1970), which is the need to ensure that the innovation takes place within a coherent framework. Mayhew (1976) also found "generally agreed-upon institutional purposes" to be an important factor leading to educational innovation. In the Rand study (Berman and Pauley, 1975), an innovation's "lack of clarity" was found to be one of the three most significant implementation problems. Finally, Miller (1974) asserts that "casual procedures for administration and dissemination" of faculty evaluation data are one of the most common reasons for failure of faculty evaluation systems. In sum, then, the more clearly the purposes and uses of the proposed faculty evaluation system can be stated, the better.

Centralized Institutional Decision Making. The degree of centralization was directly related to project success. Consistent policies and procedures were considerably harder to develop in institutions characterized by decentralized decision-making authority (that is, with a concentration of power at the dean and department-chairman levels).

Interestingly, this variable is referred to somewhat less often in the literature on organizational change. Maguire (1977) notes that the "multiconstiuency character" of colleges does tend, in general, to make adoption of innovation more difficult. The problems inherent in gaining adoption under these conditions are well illustrated in a study reported by Pressman and Wildavsky (1973). They describe how a certain urban renewal program designed to create jobs for minorities in New York City required the cumulative agreement of seventy different people or agencies. Even assuming a probability of .95 that each party would agree to the proposal *individually,* the cumulative probability of gaining endorsement of all seventy would be only .00395.

Mayhew (1976) found centralized decision making to be an important factor, but one that had inconsistent effects on the adoption of innovation. While he found that, as a rule, "the more centralized an organization's authority the *less innovative* it will be" (p. 39, emphasis added), he also found authority was concentrated in "strong and charismatic" presidents during the most creative periods in some institutions. A plausible conclusion might be that centralization has different effects, depending on the stage of the implementation process: decentralization early might be the best way to stimulate wide involvement and to encourage creative thinking; centralization later might be best to fashion a single coherent policy.

In conclusion, the preceding may be considered a list of "readiness factors" for changing an evaluation system. Colleges and universities fortunate enough to have most or all of these factors made the most progress in the SREB project.

Administrative Strategies for Change

As noted in the preceding section, the most critical factor in a successful strategy for changing a faculty evaluation program is administrative support. Although the manner in which an administrator provides support can vary from institution to institution, the style used must be consistent with his or her customary behavior. If an administrator is seen as being "authoritarian" in his or her everyday dealings with faculty members and colleagues, a sudden decision to be "democratic" will not be seen as a sincere move. Either style, however, can be accommodated in helping to bring about changes in the evaluation process. A review of the SREB project shows three styles that stand out: the administrator as director, administrator as team member, and administrator as sponsor.

Administrator as Director. If a strong leadership style is accepted within the institution and if the administrator is sufficiently respected by the faculty, it is possible for the administrator to chair the change committee and successfully guide the development of a new evaluation system. In one situation observed during the SREB project, a college dean acknowledged the need for a new, more systematic approach to faculty evaluation, appointed a committee that he chaired, and guided the development of a new system over a two-and-a-half-year period. In that situation, the administrator was fully accepted by the committee members; moreover, he was very knowledgeable about evaluation approaches and wisely brought in outside resources to provide information and expertise required by the faculty. The new system instituted at that college was thorough and comprehensive and was accepted by the majority of the faculty members. Of the thirty institutions in the project, this was perhaps the most sweeping reform implemented, since it took into account every aspect of evaluation, and it included the development of detailed rating forms and weighting systems to interrelate the various components of the evaluation systems.

Administrator as Team Member. Another approach is for an administrator to foster an atmosphere that permits his or her involvement and participation as an "equal among colleagues." This tends to emphasize the importance of the activity, and it allows the administrator to express opinions in an unofficial capacity along with faculty members working on the project.

The use of a campus team is an effective way of reviewing and redesigning faculty evaluation. The team concept implies that the group has been established for a specific purpose and that the roles of the participants are defined only by the tasks to be performed rather than by their positions in the institution. If the administrator remains a member of a team, he or she must function just as the others do, filling the roles required in order to accomplish the individual tasks. Several institutions in the SREB project successfully adopted and implemented new systems through such procedures.

In one institution, the dean who participated in the project was new to the institution. His involvement as a team member provided an opportunity for at least a small group of faculty members to get to know him quite well, to gain an understanding of his thinking about evaluation, and to learn why the administration felt this undertaking was important. It is not easy for an administrator to relinquish the position of authority and become an equal on a team. But if this is consistent with the style of the administrator and is respected by the faculty, it is an effective way to develop rapport and gain acceptance for an issue that is clearly important to the administration.

Administrator as Sponsor. In this role, the administrator takes the position that the development of the change strategy and the resulting system to be adopted and implemented is a faculty matter and one that should be left to faculty efforts. However, the administrator provides a continuing foundation for the work by supporting the team or committee with necessary time off; by providing resources, such as consultants, materials, or travel that might be required; and by providing active and visible support for the entire undertaking. The team at one institution in the SREB project included faculty members from several colleges across a large university. The team was continually aware of the support of the vice-president, who allowed time for one team member to serve as chair of the committee and continued to offer support for the team through memoranda, comments at faculty meetings, and continual personal encouragement. The end result of this undertaking was a (1) revised system that essentially clarified differences across the various colleges within this university and (2) agreement from the vice-president that differences in recommendations from the separate units would be respected in university-wide deliberations.

Approaches for Faculty Involvement

In the preceding examples of administrative strategies, the assumption was made that faculty must also be involved in any attempt to change and improve an evaluation system. There are a number of provisions that administrators can make to involve faculty in the change process. These relatively simple procedures have been identified and proved through our earlier work and in other projects that have resulted in improved and successful faculty evaluation procedures.

Careful Selection of Team Members. When selecting team participants, administrators should consider the standing of individuals among their peers, the need for representation from various parts of the institution, and above all, the importance of selecting persons who are deeply interested in the subject and committed to improving the evaluation process.

Sufficient Time for Team Members to Work on the Project. If the faculty members on the team carry heavy teaching loads, chair departments, or sit on important policy committees for the institution, little progress is likely. In selecting the team, the administrator must be sure the participants will have the necessary time to perform effectively. Even if it is not feasible to release faculty from classes, they should be temporarily relieved of other pressing institutional responsibilities.

An Appropriate Time Frame to Complete the Project. Careful planning is necessary to determine an appropriate deadline for completion. While enough time must be allowed to accomplish the task, too much time will tend to cause the issue to become stale, the team members will lose their enthusiasm, and a successful outcome will be unlikely.

Interaction with All Faculty Members at Key Points. With administrative guidance, the evaluation team should prepare position papers for review by all faculty members and periodically should hold open hearings as tentative decisions are made. When a new element of the system is designed, it should be tested in the field. When the team's work is complete, implementation should occur on a small scale or step by step to see how the program will work before it is implemented throughout the institution.

Visits to Other Successful Institutions and Attendance at Evaluation-related Conferences. Administrators should encourage travel by team members to other institutions that are known to have successfully operating evaluation programs. It is also important to send representatives to appropriate conferences relating to faculty evaluation, especially given the large number of conferences on evaluation techniques, strategies for developing programs, and examples of the ways in which evaluation systems can work.

Use of Outside Consultants. Consultation from persons outside the institution can have a major impact, especially during difficult periods in the team process. The members on the review team should know that if they need help, expertise, or mediation, it will be possible to bring someone in to help resolve a problem or make suggestions.

The Necessary Range of Resource Materials. Since faculty evaluation is not a matter with which mc.t faculty members have had to deal, they may not be aware of resources that are quite well known to administrators. The administrator should share all information that he or she has from wider contacts and should make resource materials available for the faculty review team.

Guidelines for Implementing Change

Strategies for making changes and procedures for developing new approaches must also address the requirements of implementation. The following guidelines will help administrators anticipate the implementation of new faculty evaluation programs:

1. Constant attention should be given to the feasibility of future implementation of new procedures as they are being developed. Will the structure required for operation be overly complex? Will the new plan require resources the institution cannot provide, such as computer time or the printing and processing of new forms? Will the implementation require funding that is not available, and will it be possible to obtain this funding?

2. Will the change in the system require training for those who are going to implement it? For example, many systems put a great deal of responsibility on the department chairpersons for evaluating, interpreting results, and providing help to persons who need development. Are department chairpersons ready to assume such responsibilities? Will special training be required, and, if so, how will it be developed and supported?

3. The administrator must anticipate the inevitable political problems that tend to arise in changing an existing system. Concern must be exercised for those who might be affected adversely by such changes.

4. Provisions must be made for negotiating conflicts that may arise in changing systems or implementing new procedures. It is possible, for example, that new approaches will permit different policies and procedures among units within the institution, or a new approach may foster differences in evaluation based on variations in faculty assignments. Ob-

viously, these differences will require resolution of conflicts between units and between committees and faculty members who have been allowed to use new criteria. Radically different philosophies may be at work in different parts of the institution, and it is important to consider those differences during the decision-making process.

5. Once the new system is designed, the administrator must anticipate the need for modification and adjustment before it is implemented. No form of evaluation is perfect, and, indeed, any system must undergo continual evolution.

References

Berman, P., and Pauley, E. *Federal Programs Supporting Educational Change. Vol. 2: Factors Affecting Change Agent Projects.* Santa Monica, Calif.: Rand Corporation, 1975.

Conrad, C. F. "A Grounded Theory of Academic Change." *Sociology of Education*, April 1978, *51* (2), 101–112.

Havelock, R., and others. *Planning for Innovation Through Dissemination and Utilization of Knowledge.* Ann Arbor, Mich.: Institute for Social Research, 1970.

Maguire, J. D. "Can Change Be Institutionalized? How?" *Liberal Education*, 1977, *63* (4), 584–589.

Mayhew, L. B. *How Colleges Change: Approaches to Academic Reform.* Palo Alto, Calif.: Stanford University School of Education, 1976.

Miller, R. I. *Developing Programs for Faculty Evaluation.* San Francisco: Jossey-Bass, 1974.

O'Connell, W. R., and Smartt, S. H. *Improving Faculty Evaluation: A Trial in Strategy.* Atlanta: Southern Regional Education Board, 1979.

Pressman, J., and Wildavsky, A. *Implementation.* Berkeley: University of California Press, 1973.

Watson, G. "Resistance to Change." In W. G. Bennis, K. D. Berne, and R. Chin (Eds.), *The Planning of Change.* (2nd ed.) New York: Holt, Rinehart and Winston, 1961.

William R. O'Connell, Jr., is vice-president of the Association of American Colleges. Prior to joining AAC in 1979, he was director of undergraduate education reform at the Southern Regional Education Board.

Jon F. Wergin is associate professor of the Educational Planning and Development Program at the Medical College of Virginia, Virginia Commonwealth University. He served as an evaluator for the Southern Regional Education Board's project on faculty evaluation between 1977 and 1979.

*"Incidentally, the committee didn't grant you
tenure. We'll discuss it later when I have the
time." The young professor, unprepared for what
he had just heard, was left standing in the hall as
his chairman turned and disappeared behind the
closed door to his office.*

The Chairman:
Product of Socialization
or Training?

John M. Bevan

In spite of all the oratory and argument surrounding faculty evaluation,
every professional in academe recognizes that someone does make an official judgment of professors at least once a year, if not more frequently.
Everyone knows that the individual designated to carry out this function
is the chairperson; it says so in his or her description of responsibilities.
We know also that what is recommended to the chairperson's superiors is
likely to be supported by them. What may not be understood as clearly is
that chairpersons themselves are probably very apprehensive about how
their decisions influence those they have judged favorably or harshly,
about how their decisions affect the workings of the department, about
the overall effects their critical input will have on their and others' relationships within the department and how these will affect the chairperson's own image and well-being. What is not as well perceived, and it is
best that it is not, is the fact that chairpersons are as apprehensive about
evaluation as are their colleagues on the faculty.

     Recently, South Carolina's State Personnel Department an-
nounced a new policy that directed agency heads to introduce a program
of annual review for all professional personnel, including all tenured

G. French-Lazovik (Ed.). *New Directions for Teaching and Learning:
Practices that Improve Teaching Evaluation*, no. 11 San Francisco: Jossey-Bass, September 1982.

faculty, all chairpersons, all deans and vice-presidents. In addition, a summary rating of 1 to 9 was to be given each evaluatee with percentage increments in salary correlating closely with ratings. In carrying out this assignment, one vice-president scheduled the review of department chairpersons to coincide with their review of departmental colleagues. The reaction of department chairpersons was aggravated apprehension, as evidenced by such questions as: "Would not tenured faculty, resentful of this indignity, take offense and use the occasion to strike out at their chairpersons?" "Would not this sort of synchronizing of evaluation set the stage for an exaggerated reaction, whereas a schedule that separated the evaluation of chairpersons and their colleagues might produce only slight altercations?" "You tell me, how can a colleague who has never served as a chairperson make valid appraisals of a chairperson's role and performance in budget preparation, recruitment, faculty development, faculty evaluation, research, and institutional policies?" The instance of a time schedule, which had chairpersons evaluating colleagues when colleagues were evaluating them, produced heightened reactions in chairpersons, senior staff members tenured for longer than ten years, revealing apprehensive feelings which indicated that they were unable to admit to themselves the fact that they *were accepted* by their closest associates with whom they had regularly shared confidences. Goblins were loose and on the prowl, encouraging suspicion and avoidance glances.

The reactions of the chairpersons in this setting weren't too different from those observed in young tenure-track colleagues worried about their chances of being awarded tenure. At the time young faculty members complete their advanced degrees and take teaching positions, they are only beginning the career-long process of becoming fully competent professional teachers, advisors, evaluators, committee workers, educational philosophers, and researchers. New faculty members need guidance in order to develop the skills essential to carrying out effectively these critical responsibilities. Unfortunately, these skills and the expertise related to them are acquired too frequently as the result of a process of socialization, not training (Bevan, 1974; Morgan, 1979).

So, too, with chairpersons: with little warning and a few vague charges they are initiated into an administrative position only to find themselves facing decisions on faculty evaluation, faculty recruitment, faculty development, salary increases, new-program consideration, faculty morale, the legal dimensions of personnel policy, mid-career changes, research proposals and funding, analyses of departmental and institutional goals, faculty contention, fiscal and long-range budgeting, and the protection of faculty rights and privileges. Furthermore, accompanying these new concerns is the sense that from somewhere high above someone is scrutinizing every decision. Regretfully, new skills and expertise are acquired in the same fashion as those of young instructors coveting tenure—as the result of a process of socialization, not training.

The Chairperson as the Janus Figure

The chairperson's feelings of confusion and anxiety are accentuated further by the ambiguous role of the positions. As Robert Scott (1981) points out, it is not clear what "being first among equals means"—that is, what does it mean to be department administrator and, at the same time, a full-fledged faculty member among faculty members? To be sure, as soon as you become "The Chairperson," you recognize changes taking place in your colleagues' reactions; they become a bit more reserved in your presence, their conversations become abbreviated, and the expression "between you and me" serves more frequently as the beginning of private discussions. You are the faculty member who is expected to maintain and enhance the department's position and prestige within the institution, yet you also serve as the "leader" who oversees the repair of typewriters and all other items of a nitty-gritty nature. You are counselor and friend, providing always an appropriate and fair distribution of rewards, while trying to direct and critically evaluate performance. You are a scholar trying to preserve the professional reputation that may have served as the primary distinction for your appointment as chairperson. You are the statistician working the numbers and the dollars while giving full attention to the goals and objectives of the department and the institution.

In other words, to the department, the chairperson is the Janus figure, the portal of beginnings and endings, the teacher and scholar, manager and leader, faculty member and administrator, developer and evaluator. Acting in so many roles creates confusion and anxiety in both chairperson and colleagues, but these same roles also give the chairperson a comprehensive view and broadened perspective by which to judge the progress of the department, and they provide the opportunity to become sensitized to the strengths and weaknesses of these very colleagues who determine a department's effectiveness and quality. The chairperson is the figure of conflict or ambivalence, approached easily or hesitantly, whose engagement with colleagues moves the department either forward or backward.

A key to the chairperson's primary engagement with departmental colleagues is faculty evaluation, particularly when he or she perceives such a process as vital to faculty development. When evaluation is seen as reinforcing personal growth and instructional improvement throughout faculty members' careers, then the primary goals of faculty evaluation are identical with those of faculty development—namely, the improvement of faculty teaching and the improvement of student learning. In a broader sense, such evaluation means guiding the growth of faculty members of all ages and ranks in ways exemplary of the qualities a college or university seeks to inculcate and cultivate. Unfortunately, in the minds of too many college professors evaluation is perceived as punitive and is regarded as an infringement on privacy, yet this attitude is strangely unbecoming in persons who daily devote themselves to developing critical skills and judgment in others and who regularly gauge the progress of their charges by the refinement of these critical abilities.

Without a doubt, the manner in which faculty evaluation is introduced has left much to be desired and has elicited anxiety and suspicion that cannot be dismissed as mere figments of inflamed imaginations. Case after case provides testimony of abuse inflicted by peers and patriarchs. More than likely, however, the apprehension arises from the absence in the academic setting of an evaluation process that is regularly scheduled, systematically defined, seriously pursued, and appropriately reinforced. For instance, fear and antagonism must be expected when evaluation is scheduled at intervals as infrequent as tenure and promotion reviews and with outcomes so far reaching as to eclipse an entire career. When seen and used primarily in a formative way, designed to identify and develop talent, evaluation is a stimulus to growth and is personally reinforcing. Furthermore, it is institutionally supportable because a primary objective of any administration is to identify and develop talent as early as possible, to nourish it, and to rally those who possess it so as to exploit, judiciously, their potential. Evaluation helps to uncover talent and potential not previously recognized and to direct persons richly endowed into more productive avenues.

The Chairperson as the Cornerstone to Effective Evaluation

Chairpersons are the cornerstone to effective evaluation. Most of them suspect this is true; too few want to believe it. Chairpersons spend an inordinate amount of time seeing to it that departmental supplies are replenished, class schedules and load assignments arranged, equipment ordered, and staff replacements secured, but they find very few moments to sit with a colleague to discuss innovative teaching approaches, to inquire about ongoing research, or to pass on a compliment for a committee assignment well executed. Job descriptions placed in the appropriate journal or bulletin typically define the chairperson's responsibilities as those of managing departmental business affairs, representing his or her unit to the dean, assigning classes, arranging work loads, and recruiting. Little reference is made to monitoring the development of colleagues and keeping them informed of their progress. Why do these job descriptions avoid mentioning the most important and critical responsibility, that of conducting annual and summary reviews of colleagues that tell them how well they are doing and in what ways they can best serve? Why is it so difficult to sit down with colleagues to review their performances and to use the evaluation procedure to assist them in career development? Why, during a time of retrenchment, do chairpersons and their colleagues appear to become strangers to each other? Presumably, there are as many answers to these questions as there are chairpersons.

What is important, whether it be during retrenchment or expansion, is to be sure that interview evaluation sessions do take place regularly and particularly with those faculty members whose careers are just beginning, who welcome forthright feedback, and who need to feel acknowledged and accepted, if by no other person than the department chairperson. The story can be told over and over again of persons coming up for tenure and being told for the first time in a six-year probationary period that their performance did not meet the "level of expectancy in the department" or the "level of quality set by the institution." Letters that concisely and summarily state that "it is in the best interest of the institution that your contract not be renewed" are startling, cold, and shattering. If formative counseling were an every-semester or every-year experience, carefully pursued by every department chairperson, there would be much less need for these shattering letters, and the chances for better instruction and better programs would improve. Yet this process, so essential to formative development, tends to be avoided both by chairpersons and faculty members alike.

Most critical to the process of evaluation, then, is how department chairpersons perceive their responsibilities to assist colleagues to develop in relation to the goals and objectives of the department and the university as well as what they understand about academic career development and how it correlates with institutional development. For instance, in the liberal arts setting, chairpersons need to see their departmental colleagues as resource persons (Bevan, 1978) and not merely as specialists working within the narrow confines of their own research and sub-discipline courses. After all, the institutional goals within the liberal arts undergraduate setting are much broader than those of professional and graduate schools which yield attitudes and structures supportive to the assumptions of the separate discipline; that is, only major students who have gone far enough up the incline can profit from work with the specialist. In contrast, the liberal learning concept presents a faculty member as a resource, not as someone who fills only a special slot and is constantly on the alert for competent candidates capable of achieving professional status within the respective discipline. Instead, the primary assumption is that the geneticist grows out of the biologist, grows out of the scientist, grows out of the total human being. This attitude provides rich and diverse opportunities for the specialist to learn to relate his or her knowledge, skills and expertise as a whole human being to the skills, knowledge and expertise of other human beings from different disciplines. The specialist's contribution is never ignored, nor is he denied full access to teaching and research within his or her specialty. What is expected is participation coherent with the conception of the university as a community enterprise that is directed by a philosophy of unity. The basic contrast in attitudes here is not between the generalist and the specialist but between differing models of human development. Having the appropriate model in focus is very important in evaluation if we adhere to the premise that the lives of the learned are expected to show how knowledge is related to wisdom, and that learning does enhance humanity; how the quality of education is related to the quality of life and the departmental goals do relate to institutional goals.

As department chairperson, then you need to be clear about the institution's mission and its goals because the next time you interview a candidate, you may find yourself expounding on one or another model of development; you may even appear as a witness for the defense where the model you represent has an impact on legal action. Or, when you sit down to talk with a colleague about his or her performance, you have an open invitation to talk to this person about the broad perspectives of the university as these relate to the department and as these then are reflected in what is offered in any departmental course. The person's development is pivotal to the growth and development of the institution, and it is imperative that some understanding of how these relationships translate into expectancies be reached. This development requires conversation and direction by the department chairperson; conversing informally on some regularly scheduled basis about subjects relevant to growth represents the most successful antidote to faculty confusion, anxiety, and the perception of evaluation as a punitive experience.

Annual Evaluation: Developing Effective Professors

The best opportunities available for constructive conversations cluster around the annual evaluation, which is finalized typically in an appraisal letter written by the department chairperson and to which may be attached comprehensive ratings of teaching effectiveness, professional growth and development, and contributions of an academic or professional character outside the classroom. Such conversations are enhanced if each candidate is responsible for maintaining an up-to-date dossier containing data that establish his or her effectiveness as a teacher (particularly if the data are as factual and objective as possible); (2) if the questions posed can also be supported by factual and objective data; and (3) if the faculty member perceives that the one rendering judgment is as free as possible of bias and is truly interested in the faculty member's career development.

In the area of teaching effectiveness alone the primary question is,

"What degree of success has my colleague achieved and maintained in order to be considered a good teacher?" But in answering this question, five other questions must be asked, and the answers to them sought from specific materials in the dossier prepared for submittal to the department chairperson. (These five questions, suggested dossier materials, and points of focus in examining them are taken from a peer review form prepared by French-Lazovik, 1979, and later published in a modified form, French-Lazovik, 1981.)

I. What is the quality of the teaching materials used?

Materials	*Focus in Examination of Materials*
• Course outline	• Are materials current?
• Syllabus	
• Reading list	• Are materials the best work in the
• Text	field?
• Study guide	• Are materials appropriate to the
• Description of nonprinted materials	course goals, departmental goals, institutional goals?
• Hand-outs	
• Problem sets	• Is coverage of course content
• Assignments	superficial or deep?

II. What kind of intellectual tasks were set for the students?

Materials	*Focus in Examination of Materials*
• Copies of graded exams	• What was the level of intellectual performance achieved?
• Examples of graded research papers	• What kind of work was given
• Examples of feedback to students on written work	an A?
• Grade distributions	• Did students learn what the department curriculum expected?
• Descriptions of students performance, (such as class presentations)	• Did teacher encourage students to take initiative for their own learning?
• Examples of completed assignments	

III. Has this person assumed responsibilties related to the department's or college's teaching mission?

Materials	*Focus in Examination of Materials*
• Record of service on committees, councils, honors, programs, etc.	• To what extent has this person become a departmental or college citizen in regard to teaching responsibilities?

26

- Design of course materials for special courses and programs

- What was this person's role in relevant committee work?
- Was this person appointed or elected to committee assignments?
- Is the involvement of this person appropriate to his or her academic rank?

IV. How successful is this faculty member in the classroom?

Materials

- Objective results of standardized student evaluation questionnaires of teaching, administered according to standard procedures, of teaching from several courses over several semesters
- (Do not include results from individual, faculty-made questionnaires.)
- (Do not include information based on infrequent visitation of colleague's classes.)

Focus in Examination of Materials

- Do students perceive this teacher as average or above?
- In what type of courses does he or she do best?
- What are the trends over time—that is, are there signs of improvement in skills and substantive aspects?

V. How committed to achieving excellence in teaching is this person?

Materials

- Factual statement of activities to improve teaching
- Examples of questionnaires used for formative purposes
- Examples of changes made on the basis of feedback

Focus in Examination of Materials

- Has this person sought feedback about teaching quality, explored alternative teaching methods, made changes to increase student learning?
- Has this person sought aid in trying new teaching ideas, such faculty development grants or release time to develop new courses?

If the department chairperson has carefully reviewed these data, taken notes and recorded questions to be pursued during an arranged exchange, and if both the chairperson's and colleague's attitudes toward each other are open and forthright, then such conversations can be supportively critical. Weaknesses should never be brushed over nor goals unattained ignored.

After conducting an annual interview a chairperson wrote this letter to her colleague, a tenured professor whose performance during the recent semesters had been slipping:

Dear Mark:

After reviewing your dossier, I am pleased to see that during the past year you've had several accomplishments I would like to acknowledge. One was your publication in *New Dimensions* of an article you co-authored; another was your election as president of the College's Chapter of Phi Beta Kappa. And I noticed, also that you've been active at the State level in efforts to change teacher certification.

Mark, it is my sincere hope that you will accept the comments I am about to make in the spirit that they are intended, for I want very much to facilitate, in any way I can, some changes in your performance that would eventuate in the kind of first-rate contributions to the Department and the College that you have made in the past.

From the student evaluations of your teaching, it is clear that they judge highly your ability to elucidate difficult material in their texts and to give meaningful answers to the questions they raise in class. Those ratings you must have found rewarding. On the other hand, the students' evaluation of your overall teaching effectiveness is below the average compared to both the Department and the College as a whole. This year's results continue the downward slide in your evaluations that first began two years ago.

You object, I know, to submitting course syllabi, samples of examinations, and other teaching materials requested of all faculty. If you would think about this issue from my point of view, you would undoubtedly agree that such materials give me the opportunity to make some suggestions that might be worthy of your consideration.

A number of your students commented that your classes are frequently dismissed early, by as much as an hour for a two hour and 45 minute class and that the first class is dismissed after 20 minutes. One has to wonder whether you are effectively utilizing classtime. You are not the only faculty member who has dismissed students after a few minutes of the first class period. I am well aware that certain faculty do this habitually. However, this particular behavior is something the administration has justifiably been trying to alter, and in this case, the Student Government Council supports the administration's efforts. The first class affords a wonderful opportunity for creating enthusiasm for the course as well as for establishing clearly the course expectations.

In regard to your professional growth, no one doubts that you have a mastery of the content of your discipline, but there has been no evidence of your interaction with other scholars in your field. Most scholars find such interaction stimulating to their own productivity. You know, of course, that funds are available to support faculty development and research. It is clear that other members of the Department who have used these funds have benefited, and I strongly urge you to take advantage of the faculty research funds. Any of the activities for which they may be used would contribute to your own professional growth.

Another matter centers on your schedule. Certainly, one of the advantages of our profession is the flexibility with which we can schedule our activities, and being on campus does not ensure productivity. However, it has been noted that you leave campus regularly by 2:00 P.M. and that you are frequently out of the office completely on Fridays. Given the class schedules of a number of our graduate students, it is understandable when they say it is difficult for them to obtain your help. Keep in mind that they see you as having expertise that would be of value to them.

Mark, you recall that in past years I have recommended merit raises for you, but this year I do not feel justified in recommending one. There is no doubt that you have the potential for contributing significantly more than you are now doing. My desire has been to be as straightforward as possible with you in this matter, trusting that you will reciprocate by joining in a discussion with me of the problems mentioned in this letter toward the goal of having you return to that level of contribution that characterized your work in the past. Let me say again, I stand ready to help you in any way I can.

Sincerely,

Ellen
Department Chairperson

The author of this letter has carefully observed the general guidelines for writing letters of evaluation to faculty. She began and ended the letter on a positive note. When calling attention to aspects of performance that needed to be improved, she was specific as to what relative deficiencies in performance were perceived. She acknowledged extenuating circumstances that might relate to a less than adequate performance, and she tried to identify ways the faculty member might improve his performance. While the focus was on recent performance, she looked for trends over years, not simply performance in a given year. This letter, as admitted by its author, may appear a bit harsh, but she was attempting to prick a person who was, from all appearances, beginning to enjoy the "mellowing" process. Perhaps the biggest danger in a chairperson's evaluation letter is the tendency to say only positive things and to leave the negative ones unsaid. The inevitable retort at some later time is, "But no one, neither my chairperson nor anyone else, ever said my performance was less than satisfactory!"

Worksheets for annual faculty evaluation have been designed to assist department chairpersons (1) in evaluating each faculty member in as rational and consistent a manner as possible and (2) in counseling the faculty member about strengths and weaknesses, accomplishments and shortcomings that emerge during the study of the data submitted. Gibson (and others, 1980) suggests the following procedure for the use of such worksheets:

Let it be understood that, in defining instruments and a procedure for conducting annual evaluations, we have not answered the question of what in fact constitutes an effective teacher. It would be impossible to include all pertinent ingredients in the correct amounts or even to agree upon which criteria should be selected and in what priority. What we have here is an operational definition—a model—and the suggested tools to assess each faculty member according to this model. (Perhaps we might be able to define an "effective teacher" more precisely if we could also define an "educated student"!)

Maintaining and Enhancing Effective Professors

While annual evaluations are primarily formative, tenure and promotion evaluations are summative in nature. Certainly, approaches of a formative nature can and should be incorporated in these other evaluation processes. What is absent, however, is the discussion of potential—that is, the assessment of talent and skills based on estimated outcomes. The question for tenure is what has been accomplished to date as exhibited by a candidate's performance, its consistency, and its level of quality according to stated criteria. Has he or she earned, or can he or she make a case for, a more permanent place in the faculty? Not only is retention the focus; the tenure evaluation should confirm "covenant" whereby the faculty member commits himself or herself to continue to perform in like

ANNUAL EVALUATION WORKSHEET

Study the dossier prepared by the faculty member. On the
basis of that data, and other data available to you
select for each criterion a rating that falls in the
highest category (9 or 8 on the number scale), in
the intermediate category (6,5,or 4), or the lowest
category (2 or 1). Further indicate the degree to
which the descriptions apply by circling one of the
rating numbers. These sheets need not be turned
in with the annual evaluation letter, but the
Summary Rating Sheet should be submitted to the
Dean and should be signed by both the evaluatee
and the chairperson. After making your designations,
write an annual letter of the evaluation. This written
statement will be available to the evaluatee for his/
her reaction and should serve as the focus for a
formative interview with the evaluatee. For future
salary increment consideration, a rating of 9 to 1
is given. Annual statements and summary ratings are
provided to each evaluatee and are on file both
in the department chairperson's and the dean's office.

TEACHING EFFECTIVENESS

NAME:_____

YEAR:_____

	9 8	6 5 4	2 1
Materials used by this faculty member were	of highest quality: evidence of exception- al skill in planning and organizing courses to accomplish stated goals.	of good quality: evidence of sound planning and good organi- zation to accomp- lish stated goals	inadequate: little evidence of plan- ning and organi- zation.
Intellectual tasks set for the students by this faculty mem- ber were	exceptionally well selected and evaluat- ed: excellent exams and assignments.	well selected and evaluated: good exams and assignments.	poorly selected and evaluated: exams and assign- ments not well designed.
Contributions to curriculum develop- ment by this faculty member were	of highest quality: regular source of good ideas and effective at imple- menting them.	of adequate quality: occa- sionally made useful suggest- ions for improve- ments; assisted in implementing them.	marginal: rarely showed interest in curriculum development.

	9 8	6 5 4	2 1
Student rating of this faculty member were	usually superior: generally perceived as an excellent teacher.	usually good: generally perceived as a good teacher.	marginal: indicative of serious problems as a teacher.
Attempts to improve teaching were	outstanding: showed active concern for improving teaching; sought feedback on teaching and implemented new teaching strategies.	adequate: occasionally sought feedback on, and showed evidence of concern for, improving teaching.	marginal: showed little or no interest in improving teaching.

PROFESSIONAL GROWTH AND DEVELOPMENT

	9 8	6 5 4	2 1
Scholarly activities and productivity of this faculty member were.	usually high: extensively involved in scholarly project(s); noteworthy publications; assumed prime responsibility for securing research grant.	adaquate: involved in scholarly projects; professional publications and/or presentations; assisted in securing research grant.	marginal: little or no scholarly activity; no publications or presentations of a professional nature.
Professional training activities of this faculty member were	unusually high: significantly involved in professional meetings; short courses; workshops or conferences.	adequate: attends professional meetings; short courses; workshops or conferences.	marginal: little or no imvolvement in professional training activities.
Professional recognition of this faculty member appeared to be	exceptionally good: recipient of a major professional award; invited to present papers at recognized forums; invited to referee works submitted for publication; major consultancies; elected as officer in a national, regional or state professional organization.	good: invited to review published works; minor consultancies; elected as an officer in a local professional organization.	marginal: no evidence of recognition by professional colleagues.

PROFESSIONAL SERVICE TO THE ACADEMIC COMMUNITY

	9 8	6 5 4	2 1
Contributions to the department were	outstanding: played a key role in the conduct of departmental business; volunteered for departmental responsibilities; helped to improve departmental morale.	adequate: attended departmental meetings and participated in departmental business.	inadequate: did not participate and showed little interest in departmental affairs; uncooperative; had negative impact on departmental morale.
	9 8	6 5 4	2 1
Contributions to the College were	outstanding: regularly participated in faculty meetings; made a major contribution on a College committee; active in official College functions; served as an advisor to a student group; enhanced the image of the College of professional appearances before, and cooperation with, community groups.	adequate: regularly attended faculty meetings and other official College functions; served on a College committee.	inadequate: did not attend faculty meetings regularly; showed little interest in campus affairs.
	9 8	6 5 4	2 1
Impact on colleagues was	exceptionally positive: actively participated in the professional development of others by discussing research and teaching; worked harmoniously with colleagues in solving problems.	positive: worked well with others; occasionally discussed teaching and research with others.	negative: showed no interest in the professional development of others; did not work well with others.

SUMMARY OF ANNUAL EVALUATION OF

NAME:_____

DATE:_____

Circle appropriate number

1. Teaching Effectiveness   9 8 6 5 4 2 1

2. Professional Growth and   9 8 6 5 4 2 1
   Development

3. Professional Service to   9 8 6 5 4 2 1
   the Academic Community

   SUMMARY RATING   9 8 6 5 4 2 1

Signatures:

_____   _____
Evaluatee   Date

_____   _____
Department Chairperson   Date

_____   _____
Dean/School   Date

fashion and the institution commits itself to support the faculty member in like fashion within the limits of mission and fiscal responsibility.

Promotion, on the other hand, is based on merit performance measured by the accomplishments attainable for a respective rank designation. The question here is, "What more has he or she done than all, or most all, of the others of that rank to be deserving of such recognition?"

Put into AAUP terms, tenure represents a promise on the part of the college that it will not dismiss without cause a faculty member who has demonstrated during the probationary period satisfactory performance as a teacher, scholar, and contributor to the college community and who shows a clear indication of being an exemplar for nontenured faculty. Promotion represents recognition of meritorious service, of accomplishment above the norm.

The role of the chairperson in these models of evaluation is not too different from the role played in the annual evaluation process. It is much more formal, however, because (a) these processes are not considered developmental in thrust; (b) the chairperson is interacting not only with the candidate and dean but also with departmental and institutional review panels; (c) the materials requested of the candidate are assembled in a specified format on the order of a portfolio that provides information spanning a period of about three to five years; (d) colleagues within the department prepare working papers (confidential appraisal letters) on the candidate at the same time that questionnaires are sent to graduates who have gone on to graduate school or to work within the profession; (e) the final authority for the decision by matters unrelated to the candidate's performance. These factors add heavily to the duties of the chairperson.

Vital to the making of sound tenure decisions is the thoughtful and resolute participation in the evaluation process by departmental colleagues and department chairpersons, particularly in improving the quality of the working papers provided by colleagues (as in the above illustration) or of other forms of written colleague review. What appears in a working paper will depend largely on the seriousness with which its composer takes the responsibility and on the information on which its content is based. Department chairpersons need to emphasize repeatedly the care that should go into preparing these documents. Before writing a working paper colleagues should study the portfolio thoroughly, and the judgment rendered in the paper should be based on the data available— course syllabi, tests, reading lists, standard student evaluation summaries, performance of students on standardized tests, publications, record of attendance and presentations at professional meetings, proposals written, service on committees or in other roles of responsibility, and other relevant enclosures. The chairperson must be sure that colleagues focus their attention on common concerns. This may be done by supplying them with sets of questions to be addressed that reflect the common criteria.

Furthermore, it may be judicious for the chairperson to point out that working papers done in a perfunctory manner reflect poorly on those who write them; the quality of such letters may be reflected when the chair evaluates the writer's own departmental service.

In helping a candidate compose a portfolio, the department chairperson needs to provide guidance as to what materials are useful and appropriate to include. He or she must make it clear that portfolios should neither be fattened by reams of irrelevant data nor left so lean as to leave evaluators without sufficient persuasive information. The items enclosed should provide evidence only of competence and be as free of bias as possible. Written undergraduate student comments should not be included because, while such testimony may be revealing, its primary value is in the formative process; and considering it for summative purposes may distort, mislead, and give an inappropriate weighting to the opinions of the more vocal few or of the better writers. In short, the chairperson should prepare and distribute uniform guidelines regarding the types of materials to be included in the portfolio and their ordered sequence. A timetable would also be most helpful in getting colleagues started early enough in the writing of working papers to allow for study and reflection; in other words, let your colleagues know when the portfolio should be available for study by its reviewers, when reviewers should have completed their reading of the portfolio, when working papers should be completed and turned in, when the review panel convenes, and when the department chairperson meets with the candidate to summarize the action of the panel and to provide whatever counsel and guidance may be needed for the next steps.

The department chairperson should summarize in writing the cogent points that led to the decision made by the departmental panel, whether it be in the case of tenure or promotion. For reasons strictly legal, chairpersons have been encouraged to shy away from putting anything in writing, but, with good instructions by legal counsel as to phrasing, it should be possible for chairpersons to document the outcome of such evaluations without worrying about entrapping phases and undue jeopardy to a college or university. In fact, the chairperson should be free to assume the role of a "friend at court," to offer advice and counsel, if he feels a colleague has been unfairly judged.

Chairpersons frequently offer too little counseling prior to and after formal evaluations of tenure and promotion, perhaps because most chairpersons have limited experience and training in the managerial skills crucial to carrying out this responsibility effectively. This can be remedied by having the president or provost meet with chairpersons to emphasize orally what the faculty handbook advocates in the area of faculty development and evaluation. (A word spoken by the highest authority often carries a force that is missed in manuals that impart information about so many other mundane matters.) Faculty evaluation and counseling workshops held annually, conducted on or off campus, can be very beneficial to chairpersons and other tenured panel members who are involved in the evaluation process. Such workshops must be led by qualified, experienced consultants. Finally, the provost should meet with evaluation panel members to emphasize orally what the faculty manual prescribes regarding tenure and promotion. These and other efforts will help ensure a better understanding of the process and of everyone's role in it and will encourage more frequent exchanges within a counseling setting.

Rewarding Effective Professors

Unfortunately, the availability of counseling is inconsequential if there are not sufficient rewards to encourage the behavioral modifications suggested through evaluation. Department chairpersons and their administrative associates acknowledge that faculty members are a college's or university's primary resource for stimulating learning and that they are the central force in maintaining and enhancing its character and vitality. Administrators also agree that programs of faculty evaluation and faculty development must be given highest priority, and appropriate reward systems must be established to reinforce them. Thus, it is somewhat surprising to find so few incentives offered for the encouragement, renewal, and development of this most valuable resource. The traditional rewards are tenure, promotion, teaching-load reductions, modest salary increments, and an occasional distinguished chair.

Very little beyond promotion to full professor can be anticipated by the majority of persons who are very good in every area of scholarly endeavor but not distinguished enough to merit the infrequent rave notices dispersed by the in-house public relations organ. Somewhere the establishment has lost sight of faculty as a group of very different individuals needing varieties of incentives and opportunities to stimulate and extend potential. Faculty evaluation repeatedly substantiates this judgment, yet the rewards in response to it are standard and sterile. New approaches to reward must be explored—approaches that are oriented less toward summative processes and more toward the formative dynamic processes. No one is more responsible in bringing about these innovations than the chairperson, with the undergirding of the dean. The following paragraphs offer a few suggestions.

Research Resources Fellow. This faculty member receives release time, $2500, and modest project funds to pursue research, preferably leading to external funding. He or she also serves as a resource person for other faculty in some significant way (such as offering brownbag luncheon seminars on new issues in science, review of others' ideas for proposals, contacts with influential scholars to bring them to campus for a roundtable type of gathering). The more this kind of aid is given to faculty, particularly if it is interdisciplinary in scope, the better the odds are that the institution's purposes will be met.

Interdisciplinary Lecturer. He or she will propose a broad topic or skill that may be relevant to a wide range of courses and will make his or her availability known to colleagues, may offer lectures and demonstrations to classes and departments, and will assist in preparing syllabi where his or her expertise is needed. The recipient will receive a stipend of $2500.

Docent in Teaching. This faculty member receives release time, $2500, and some project funds to lead a seminar, workshop series, or other project related to improved teaching and acts as an in-house consultant on teaching for those who request help. He or she may concentrate on relatively theoretical issues, on concrete topics (self-paced materials, independent study, competency-based learning), or on special clientele (women, the gifted, the learning-disabled). The proposed activitiy should include a significant portion of personal study in teaching and learning research.

Faculty-Named Scholarships. Outstanding faculty members will have a student scholarship named in their honor. These will be funded by alumni, corporations, and other gift sources. They should be on the order of $1,000 or more per year.

Annual Research Award. This reward offers the faculty member a course-load reduction each semester to complete new or ongoing research and to prepare a paper for presentation at a faculty banquet in his or her honor.

Student Assistance Grants. These are grants of up to $500 requested by a faculty member for a student or students engaged in a project directed by, or a venture recommended by, the professor. The satisfaction derived by a professor upon receiving funds to provide assistance for study abroad, for research materials, or to attend a professional meeting is great. (It's too bad a portion of a student's tuition is not returned for purposes of enriching his or her academic experience. If this were possible, a new dimension would be added to the mentoring responsibilities of professors. It is conceivable that student government associations might be persuaded to make funds available for such awards recommended by professors.)

Banking Credits. Course credit overloads or hours credited for directing independent study are "banked," and when the equivalent to a semester's load has been accumulated (usually within a designated period, such as three years), the holder of the banked credits is entitled to a semester's leave for study and research. An overload in one semester may mean an equivalent load reduction in the next semester. Through this means, faculty members may secure time for writing, for working up new courses, for doing research to improve classroom instruction, or for spending additional time with students in independent study. Banking time for creative undertakings is based on dollars earned from tuition paid for hours taught and for which no extra compensation was paid.

These are merely a few of the reinforcing approaches available. Described elsewhere (Bevan, 1979) are many others: a trainer resource, in-house visiting lecturers, mini-grants, internal sabbaticals, after-tenure rewards, after-retirement rewards, and so on. Faculty members should also be recognized for the significant accomplishments of former students who attribute their distinction to the strong influence of a particular mentor. Defining a method of securing appropriate data for the selection of one or more professors in this category of rewards would be a challenge. (It might provide an answer to the young classics professor who said that it would take ten years before he could say whether any of the students presently taking courses with him were influenced by him. I had asked him about outcomes he hoped to see in his students as a result of taking his courses.)

Assessing the Assessor

In talking about department chairpersons and the evalution of faculty, we must also talk about the evaluation of chairpersons. Usually, those appointed to this position will be people who have the confidence of both the departmental faculty and the college administration. In addition, they may have charisma. However, it is unwise to expect that charisma alone will shape effectively the professional growth of entire departments. This takes, in addition to shared confidence and personal persuasion, a great deal of knowledge about planning, of professional respect, and of administrative skill.

A chairperson's evaluation includes an annual review and a five-year evaluation (if each department is required to evaluate its progress every five years and to include in that evaluation an assessment of the effectiveness of its chairperson should he or she wish to continue in that capacity). Both the annual and the five-year assessment should protect the department against the entrenched domination of an insensitive or incompetent chairperson.

The annual evaluation usually involves three elements: (1) a statement of departmental objectives, accomplishments, and projections; (2) a self-evaluation by the chairperson of his or her personal and professional development; and (3) the evaluation of administrative skills.

Just prior to the closing of the academic year, each chairperson submits a statement to his or her dean or provost setting forth goals and objectives for the coming year, provides a summary of the successes and failures of the year immediately past, and expatiates on the reasons for failures and what additional time and resources may be needed. This statement should be distributed to departmental colleagues for comment before it is submitted to and discussed with the dean. The purpose of these discussions is to highlight strengths and accomplishments, to identify programs and skills that need improvement, to agree on a timetable and on priorities, and to plan new departmental and professional strategies.

The self-evaluation phase of the annual review is conducted in the same manner and according to the same schedule as the annual review of regular faculty members. The dean acts in the role of the chairperson and prepares the annual review letter, adhering to the same guidelines and aids for composing the letter and for conducting the interview. For future salary increment consideration, a summary rating is given. John Centra (1979) and Grace French-Lazovik (1976) have analyzed well the benefits and limitations of self-analysis.

The evaluation of administrative skills introduces another scale and procedure. At the time the chairperson is preparing his annual dossier, an Evaluation of Administrative Skills questionnaire (see Figure 1) is forwarded to no fewer than twelve senior evaluators in a large department or, in a small department, to every member. In the case of the large department, six of the twelve evaluators might be named by the evaluatee and six of the twelve named by the respective dean. These questionnaires are sent out from and returned to the respective dean or the provost. (It is most helpful in the follow-up interview if the results of the questionnaire are presented in the form of a profile.) The data received are discussed with the dean or provost and, for future salary increment consideration, a rating is given. Allen Tucker (1981) provides samples of linking salary increases to ratings.

The evaluation of the chairperson gives the added opportunity of assessing a department's productivity and direction, of inducing participatory planning, and of gauging the approximation of departmental goals to institutional goals; it provides a means of assessing the most important unit (the department) and of determining how that unit relates to the whole (the college). The evaluation of the chairperson becomes a means of negotiating the maintenance and enhancement of the department.

A Concluding Comment

One last observation must be made: at the very roots of evaluation is collegiality. At a time when rumors stalk the campuses, when the suggestion of action across discipline lines is regarded as an infringement of closely guarded turf, when cooperation is embraced only after control is secured, when truth is shrouded in rules and regulation and not in the understanding among people and of people, then evaluation opens a way

Figure 1. Sample Form for Evaluation of Administration Skill

Chairperson being evaluated:

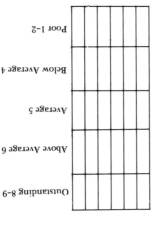

	Outstanding 8-9	Above Average 6	Average 5	Below Average 4	Poor 1-2

1. COMMUNICATIONS

1. Communications in a timely and responsive manner
2. Conducts decisive conferences and interviews
3. Balances and validates conflicting information effectively and fairly
4. Writes letters or makes statements that seldom need clarification
5. Shares important data willingly and in an organized manner
6. Communicates interest in helping faculty develop skills and expertise

2. DECISION-MAKING

7. Makes sound and timely decisions
8. Gathers pertinent facts before acting
9. Applies policy consistently and fairly
10. Is skilled in participatory decision-making
11. Shows unusual aptitude in negotiating compromise when necessary

3. PLANNING

12. Plans ahead for those activities under his/her cognizance
13. Makes time for planning by delegating routine work
14. Keeps goals up to date and clearly stated
15. Is receptive to constructive suggestions for changes
16. Encourages initiative and innovation
17. Encourages instructional improvement offers

4. OPERATIONS/ACTIONS

18. Initiates and sustains action toward defined goals
19. Assigns duties so as to maximize capabilities of those involved
20. Is skilled and knowledgeable in those specialities and areas demanded by his/her assignments
21. Works well with committees
22. Demonstrates a clear understanding of the role and scope of his/her assignments and responsibilities
23. Negotiates arrangements within the department in support of faculty development
24. Recognizes the importance of faculty evaluation and strongly supports it

5. PROBLEM SOLVING

25. Solves problems efficiently and quickly
26. Is alert to potential problems
27. Is able to cope with unanticipated events
28. Approaches problem solving on a systematic basis

6. HUMAN/PUBLIC RELATIONS

29. Gives proper and generous credit to others for their contributions
30. Strives to help those under his/her supervision develop their full potential
31. Understands the College well enough to refer matters to the proper offices for effective action
32. Constantly strives to broaden both the internal and external perception of the goals and accomplishments of the college
33. Actively supports the Affirmative Action policy of the institution

Category ratings: Communications _____
Decision Making _____
Planning _____
Operations/Action _____
Problem Solving _____
Human/Public Relations _____
Summary rating _____

Please return to Dean _____ by April 15, 1980

for sharing, trusting, and building because it provides a vehicle for conversing in a common language about common concerns and commitments. When persons are able to talk openly and critically about their professional endeavors and aspirations to colleagues who share some of the responsibility for their growth, knowing that such engagements are not free of stress and pain, then there is a chance to restore to the campus the aura of colleagueship—that is, the kind of friendship described by Norman Cousins as the oldest and most precious of the arts.

We must be able to talk in a supportively critical fashion to each other if collegiality is to regain its place in the academy, regardless of a decision to tenure or not to tenure, to promote or not to promote, to retain or not to retain. Evaluation does not provide the solution to all that is awry in academe, but it can open up new approaches to old problems. A key person in this venture may very well be the chairperson—the chairperson who is trained, and helps to train others, for the challenges confronting the system.

References

Bevan, J. M. "Faculty Development." Paper presented at the Deans' Workshop, Association of American Colleges, Estes Park, June 18, 1974.

Bevan, J. M. "Faculty Resource Pool: Mark of an Innovative Institution." *North Carolina Libraries*, 1978, *35*, 33–41.

Bevan, J. M. "Faculty Evaluation and Institutional Rewards." In W. O'Connell, Jr. (Ed.), *Improving Undergraduate Education in the South*. Atlanta, Ga.: Southern Regional Education Board, 1979.

Centra, J. *Determining Faculty Effectiveness*. San Francisco: Jossey-Bass, 1979.

Gibson, G., and others. *Report of the Committee on Evaluation of Evaluation Procedures at the College of Charleston*. Charleston, S.C.: College of Charleston, 1980.

French-Lazovik, G. "Evaluation of College Teaching." Occasional paper for the Association of American Colleges, 1976.

French-Lazovik, G. *Data on Peer Review of Teaching*. Report prepared for Office for the Evaluation of Teaching, University of Pittsburgh, November 16, 1979.

French-Lazovik, G. "Peer Review: Documentary Evidence in the Evaluation of Teaching." In J. Millman (Ed.), *Handbook of Teacher Evaluation*. Beverly Hills, Calif.: Sage, 1981.

Morgan, G. A. "Using Grants for Faculty Development." In K. Mohrman (Ed.), *Grants: Views from the Campus*. Washington, D.C.: Association of American Colleges, 1979.

Scott, R. A. "Portrait of a Department Chairperson." *AAHE Bulletin*, 1981, *33* (6), 1–6.

Tucker, A. *Chairing the Academic Department*. Washington, D.C.: American Council on Education, 1981.

John M. Bevan is executive director of the Charleston Higher Education Consortium, Charleston, S.C. He has served as provost and academic vice-president at Eckerd College, The University of the Pacific, Davidson College, and the College of Charleston. He was chairman of the steering committee for ETS's Undergraduate Assessment Program and in that capacity was a member of the GRE Board.

*In order for any faculty evaluation plan to work,
there must be a base of expertise that faculty and
administrators can draw upon.*

The Role of an
Evaluation Specialist

Grace French-Lazovik

Can a sound teaching evaluation plan be developed without drawing
upon the knowledge of a person with expertise in the field of evaluation?
Perhaps, but it is not likely. Edwin Guthrie (1954) said long ago in his
monograph that has become a classic in the field of teaching evaluation,
"successful [evaluation] requires as much experience and technical
knowledge as the construction of a broadcasting station. It is, unfortunately, harder for the amateur to tell when the results are worthless"
(p. 10).

Why Is a Specialist Needed?

Precisely because part of the evaluation enterprise entails measurement, special knowledge is needed. Evaluating a complex human
performance like teaching requires forms of psychological measurement
that pose difficult technical problems. Faculty members, for the most
part, have enough awareness of these problems to ask, "Are the data
collected reliable and valid?" But the conditions likely to produce psychometrically sound results and the methods of analysis that reveal the
degree of reliability and validity present in data are not general knowl-

G. French-Lazovik (Ed.). *New Directions for Teaching and Learning:
Practices that Improve Teaching Evaluation*, no. 11. San Francisco: Jossey-Bass, September 1982.

edge. They are the special domain of the expert in psychological measurement.

When Is an Evaluation Specialist Needed?

Countless missteps and false directions in developing or revising a teaching evaluation system can be prevented if expert advice is sought at the earliest possible point, even when discussions by faculty committees or administrators are just beginning. Often these discussions proceed in wrong directions because questions arise that require specific, informational answers. "Aren't evaluations of teachers made five or ten years after a student finishes college quite different from those made at the end of a course?" "Wouldn't peer evaluations based on classroom visitations be more reliable than student evaluations?" The journal literature on teaching evaluation contains research answers to such questions, but unless someone familiar with that literature can provide answers, discussion can ramble down blind alleys and decisions can produce wasted efforts.

The next point at which an evaluation specialist can provide important input occurs at the planning stages. Decisions must be made about the kinds of data that will be used, about the procedures for data collection, and about the policies that will govern the process. Informed plans usually produce sound and sophisticated evaluations; uninformed decisions at this crucial stage can be costly indeed, for if they produce unreliable or inaccurate results, then everyone is exposed to unfairness and its legal ramifications.

Finally, when an evaluation system is implemented, its operation should be directed by a knowledgeable specialist, preferably of faculty rank. The quality of an evaluation system largely depends on the careful handling and processing of data, the knowledge of sources of bias that can distort results and of ways to avoid those pitfalls, as well as on experience in data analysis and interpretation. But beyond these skills there must be the sense of responsibility that is part of the ethical standards of a professional—in this case, responsibility for preserving the absolute confidentiality of results, the anonymity of raters, and the integrity of the policies that govern the system. More than once, I have seen a faculty reluctant to accept evaluation procedures that were to be supervised by a committee. But when an evaluation director whom the faculty trusted was designated, much of the objection disappeared. No wonder, for it is hard to fix upon a committee, whose membership can change over time, the responsibility that is so necessary to the faculty trust that must develop if the system is to function. Unless faculty members trust the handling of a matter so vital to their professional careers, no set of evaluation procedures will work.

Where Are Evaluation Specialists Found?

On a university campus there is no shortage of people with general training in psychological measurement. They may be found in the psychology department in the area of psychological testing and measurement or in the school of education in the departments of educational research or educational psychology. There may be an evaluation research group in social psychology, occasionally in a school of business, or sometimes among support personnel in professional schools of medicine, social work, or public administration.

In a liberal arts college, however, such specialists are not likely to be found among the faculty, and even in institutions where evaluation specialists are available, few will have worked in the specific area of evaluating college teaching or will be acquainted with the rather extensive literature on the subject that has appeared in recent decades. The Southern Regional Education Board conducted a two-year project (O'Connell and Smartt, 1979) in which thirty colleges and universities reviewed and revised their faculty evaluation procedures. One of the conclusions drawn from this project offers excellent advice on the problem of where to find an evaluation specialist:

> In order for *any* faculty evaluation [plan] to work . . . there must be a base of expertise that the faculty and administration can draw upon in developing or revising their system. This expertise can come from a variety of sources, both internal and external to the institution. External resources in the form of consultants play a key role; the most successful institutions were those . . . [in the project] able to specify how a consultant could best complement their own strengths [p. 33].

Critical Questions in Developing an Evaluation System

The discussions attendant upon the development or revision of evaluation procedures at any institution bring up several common questions. An understanding of the issues relevant to these questions can reduce the amount of controversy they often precipitate. The following subsections examine a few of the more important questions and indicate some of the ways in which an evaluation specialist can contribute.

For What Purpose Will the Evaluation Results Be Used? Few faculty members or administrators realize the consequences for procedures and policies that follow upon the answer to this question. Scriven (1967) has provided a terminology that usefully differentiates the two primary purposes that evaluation serves. Used solely for improvement, *formative evaluation* has an entirely different set of requirements from *summative evaluation,* which is used for decisions of promotion or tenure. The extent of these differing requirements has been delineated by this author in another publication (French-Lazovik, 1976), so only a brief summary will be mentioned here.

The essential differences stem from the fact that if data considered in academic decisions are to contribute to fairness, they must be reliable, valid, and comparable for all those faculty members considered. Thus, certain types of data (such as those from classroom visitation by peers or from self-evaluations) cannot be used summatively. They can, however, contribute fruitfully to formative evaluation. If student evaluations of teaching are planned, the type of questionnaire, the number and nature of the items it contains, the type of response categories used by students, the frequency and mode of questionnaire administration, as well as the policies governing who sees the results—all hinge on whether the student evaluations will be used for formative, summative, or dual purposes. The essential point is that once the purpose is decided, then a whole set of questions about procedure has automatically been answered.

If a summative purpose is desired, then, in addition to collecting student perceptions of teaching, the evaluation procedure must examine those aspects of teaching that cannot be judged by students (such as a teacher's knowledge; the currentness, accuracy and quality of teaching materials; the quality of the intellectual tasks set for the students; and the level of performance achieved by them). The evaluation of those dimensions of teaching requires other methods, one of which may entail peer judgments based on review of the documentary evidence of teaching by those knowledgeable in the discipline taught (French-Lazovik, 1981). In addition, very careful procedures are necessary to eliminate the usual sources of bias in data collected from peers (see the chapters by Donald Hoyt and Kenneth Eble in this volume; Cohen and McKeachie, 1980).

Perhaps the best advice that can be offered is that the questions regarding evaluative purpose should be addressed at the outset, and the procedural consequences inherent in each purpose should be fully explored before any decision is reached.

How Will Data from Students Be Obtained? The answer here seems obvious: by the use of an individualized questionnaire (if only formative purposes are to be served), by a standardized instrument for summative use, or by a format that contains both standardized elements and also permits additional questions formulated by each teacher, if both formative and summative purposes are intended. It is the next step that brings the crucial choice—should you build your own standard instrument, borrow one (or more) developed at other institutions, or buy services from one of the organizations that provide them, such as Student Instructional Report (SIR) (Educational Testing Service), Instructional Development and Effectiveness Assessment System (IDEA) (Kansas State

University), Endeavor Instructional Rating System (EIRS) (Northwestern University), or others listed by Centra (1979). Which of these alternatives is best suited to a particular institution takes very careful consideration, and the choice must depend on the institution's needs and resources.

Building one's own evaluation form is the most difficult course, requiring high-level expertise. If the building is done well, including the work necessary to validate the instrument, there can be advantages very hard to achieve by any other means, for nothing is so much owned by a faculty as what it has created for itself. By the same token, here lies the greatest risk of a poor instrument, one that uses inappropriately scaled categories or questions on which no consensus among observers is obtained, one that produces fluctuating and unreliable results, or highly skewed distributions that do not discriminate levels of teaching merit among individuals, thus giving meaningless scores. Where there are the resources, the expertise (either internal or external), and the motivation to develop one's own instrument, it is a desirable way to proceed. A number of large universities and some liberal arts colleges have constructed sound and useful instruments of their own. However, in honesty I must admit to having seen some colleges plow ahead in uninformed confidence, producing the most awful results and remaining the least aware of their mistakes.

When building one's own instrument is contraindicated, either of the other alternatives can provide excellent instruments if the choice is made with care. Only instruments designed to serve the purpose desired should be considered. If summative use is at stake, an essential consideration should be what kind of normative data are available or will be collected. An evaluation specialist's comparative review of the psychometric properties of the instruments under consideration, as well as the appropriateness of the instrument for the particular school, can provide important input to this crucial choice.

What Policies Improve the Quality of Data from Students? Should student evaluations be required in every course, or should faculty be allowed to request student evaluations of teaching when they wish them? How frequently should student evaluations be administered? Is it better to have all courses taught in one term evaluated and not do any evaluations the second term or to evaluate half of the courses taught each term?

Here again, the purpose of the data must guide the policy. Obviously, if only formative purposes are involved, then faculty members should have full choice as to when, or whether, evaluations take place. If summative purposes are to be served, then other goals should govern the policy selected. One of the most important of these goals entails maximizing the quality of data collected. Requiring every course to be evaluated by students every term frequently contributes to deterioration in data quality, for students often experience this amount of evaluation as excessive, and they become sloppy and careless in filling out questionnaires. On the other hand, when students know that they do not always get an opportunity to express their opinions, they are more careful to give the questionnaire their full attention.

Another contributor to quality data can be the instructions given to students at the time questionnaires are administered. Do they emphasize the seriousness of the evaluation task as well as the serious attention that will be accorded the students' opinions? Administration of questionnaires by a neutral person, rather than by the instructor himself or herself, and the guarantee that results will not be reported until after final grades are in the registrar's office help assure students that their anonymity will be protected, thereby eliciting more candid responses.

Data quality is also dependent on the questionnaire format, the conditions of its administration, and a host of other measurement details that are part of a specialist's tools.

Should Student Evaluation of Teaching Be Mandatory? Governing policies addressing this question should consider not only the effect of mandatory evaluation on the quality of data but also the equally important goal of fairness, both to those being evaluated and those needing data for decisions. Summative evaluation must rest on an adequate amount of data, certainly not on students judgments from one course or even several courses in the same term. Data sufficient to determine trends, to ascertain whether improvement is demonstrated over time, are essential to fairness; thus, guidelines as to what should be available at the time of tenure consideration or promotion are needed. Much variation exists across different schools, depending on local circumstances and needs, but a few examples may help.

A policy that works well in a number of schools permits a faculty member to request student evaluations of teaching whenever he or she wishes, requiring only that one evaluation per term (or two per year) be placed in the dossier whenever undergraduate teaching is part of a faculty member's responsibilities. Some schools have a policy specifying that the dossier contain one evaluation for each *different* course taught in a two-year period. Since reappointment and tenure decisions most frequently come after three to six years, this policy allows ample time for data accumulation. Such policies provide enough freedom for faculty to risk new teaching techniques or new courses they wish to try without the deterrent of being required to place every evaluation result in the dossier.

Preserving faculty willingness to change their teaching is so essential to teaching quality that it should be carefully guarded. By its nature, college teaching must constantly change—with new content, texts, organization, research findings (some of which necessitate changes in teaching methods)— and each faculty member must risk the attendant possibility that the change, especially on its first trial, will be less successful than anticipated. A policy that strikes an equitable balance between the need for data at the time of decisions and the need to provide faculty freedom to risk change maximizes the benefits that can come from a good evaluation system. Policies of this type can be developed if the consequences for all parties concerned—faculty members, students, and administrators—are carefully considered when an evaluation system is being planned or revised.

The Need for Expertise in Reporting and Interpreting Evaluation Results

The place where lack of measurement expertise probably does the greatest harm is in summarizing, reporting, and interpreting evaluative data. The handling of quantified responses, if they are to be meaningful, imposes restrictions that the nonspecialist may not even suspect. When are data representative? What is the smallest-size class for which the pooled responses on a student evaluation instrument are interpretable? The answers to these questions depend on the technical analyses of reliability of the particular instrument in use, not on uninformed guesses.

How should the results of student evaluations of teaching be presented to faculty? Unfortunately, the procedure that is most commonly used, that of presenting item means, leads to considerable misinterpretation. It assumes that the actual scale midpoint is the same as the scale's theoretical midpoint, a condition that is almost never true. An extreme example may serve to illustrate this point. Consider the following item to which students are asked to respond on the accompanying scale:

The instructor's voice was loud enough to be heard.
1. *Rarely* (less than 20 percent of the time)
2. *Seldom* (between 20 and 40 percent of the time)
3. *About Half the Time* (between 40 and 60 percent of the time)
4. *Frequently* (between 60 and 80 percent of the time)
5. *Almost Always* (more than 80 percent of the time)

The theoretical mean of a five-point scale is 3.0, but the actual mean of this item is probably very close to 5.0 because the real frequency of this behavior is quite high. Thus, it makes little sense for an instructor whose mean rating on this item is 4.91 to compare his or her score to a mean of 3.00 and conclude that he or she is doing well above average in this respect.

The correlated assumption that the real means of all items that have the same number of response categories are equal is also untrue. It often leads faculty members to conclude incorrectly that they are doing better on one item than another, when in fact it is the item distributions that account for the differences in means.

These problems point to the need for reporting something more than raw means of quantified responses. Normative data are essential for adequate interpretation of student evaluations of teaching, but the referent sample must be representative and its size adequate. Local norms are desirable, but they cannot be broken down into such small groups that comparison becomes meaningless. It is not uncommon to encounter colleges where faculty members have insisted on departmental norms. Only in the very largest departments of the very largest universities would there be a sufficient number of faculty members for departmental norms to be interpretable, and even there much caution would be needed. For almost all schools, as well as for the smaller departments of large universities (how many faculty are typically in a classics department?), *local departmental norms are psychometrically unsound.* A much better procedure is to establish a referent sample on the items that are general enough to be appropriate across departments (such as overall teaching effectiveness, overall worth of the course) in academic units that have sufficient faculty and similarity to give meaningful comparisons, like the College of Arts and Sciences or the College of Engineering.

Some schools have provided benchmark data from student evaluations to help in the interpretation of results, such as norms for large classes versus small classes, required versus elected courses, and so on. The decision as to which benchmarks should be provided rests on discovering what variables are actually related to differences in student ratings. The widely quoted studies that imply the same variables are operating on all campuses misrepresent the data. Which variables contribute to differences depends heavily on the evaluative instrument used and on the nature of the students and faculty at a particular school. The goal in choosing a reporting system should be to present data in a way that fosters accurate interpretation by faculty and enhances their efforts to improve.

The Evaluation Director as Consultant

A very useful role that an evaluation director can play focuses on helping faculty and administrators interpret and understand the results they receive. Advice and information can be provided through written materials, through individual training sessions, or through workshops for individuals, especially department chairpersons, who will use evaluative data in decisions and recommendations. Consultation of this type contributes to faculty acceptance of a process that, by its nature, can engender massive resistance.

Some of the Most Common Errors

1. *Using in tenure and promotion considerations the results of student evaluations of teaching obtained for formative use only.* Faculty are often willing to institute a program of student evaluations of teaching with the stipulation that the results be used only formatively. It then becomes a great temptation for those who get high ratings to submit them for a summative consideration. Lacking the psychometric properties and the procedural controls necessary for validity and comparability, such use can contribute to unfair decisions.

2. *Using the same rating items for all teaching situations.* Teaching activities in courses in the performing arts, in physical education, or in clinical teaching settings are usually quite different from those in the typical classroom. Except on the most general items, such teaching is not appropriately judged based on the items that constitute most standard questionnaires.

3. *Using students' written comments summatively.* Students appreciate having the opportunity to add their own written comments after completing standard questionnaires. Often they wish to explain further the ratings they have made or to comment on unique aspects of a course. Such comments can provide useful feedback for the teacher's efforts to improve and should be for the "teacher's eyes only." Because they cannot be represented objectively and because a dramatically worded comment, even though it might be totally unrepresentative of the class's opinions, could have a devastating effect on a dean's judgment, they should have no place in academic decisions.

Quite a number of years ago, the student government board at a large university carried out their own course evaluations, publishing the results in a booklet with a little paragraph of written comments under each faculty member's name. They made no effort to see that these paragraphs were representative of all comments submitted and, in fact, especially chose the most colorful and attention-getting remarks. When two faculty members who believed they had been libeled threatened suit, the project was quickly dropped. But students are not the only ones who make this mistake. I have seen colleges where the deans or divisional chairpersons were very reluctant to give up reading all the written comments made by students, claiming that these were the only data that gave them "a feeling for what their faculty were doing." Such insensitivity to the sources of bias in data not only destroys faculty trust in the evaluation process but also invites legal challenge.

4. *Summing the item means to get an overall evaluation.* This practice assigns a weight to each item that ignores the fact that some items may be highly related to overall teaching effectiveness and some may be of far less importance (French-Lazovik, 1974). If summing is to be done

54

appropriately, very sophisticated statistical procedures are required, such as those developed by Paul Horst and used at the University of Washington from 1957–1973. An easier approach that is adequate in most instances is to include an item on the questionnaire that calls for a separate judgment of overall teaching effectiveness.

5. *Using student evaluations as the only measure of teaching.* Student evaluations are essential to provide first-hand data on what takes place in the classroom, but we cannot adequately measure the quality of teaching on the basis of student judgment alone, for there are important aspects of teaching that students are not qualified to judge.

6. *Evaluation overkill.* Once an evaluation system is put into place, there is a great temptation to use it excessively. I have seen colleges go from collecting no objective data at all to having everything in sight evaluated several times a year. Good evaluation takes time—the time of students, of faculty, and of administrators. Excessive evaluation results in a deterioration of the quality of data obtained and quickly eliminates the benefits that a good system can provide.

It is well to remember that evaluation expertise does not substitute for wisdom in administration or goodwill in faculty relations. But an expert's knowledge can help prevent the controversies that often surround the use of evaluation procedures, the unfairness that results from unsound methods, and the faculty distrust that is fostered by ignorance of the fundamental research or logic on which sound evaluation rests.

References

Centra, J. A. *Determining Faculty Effectiveness.* San Francisco: Jossey-Bass, 1979.
Cohen, P. A., and McKeachie, W. J. "The Role of Colleagues in the Evaluation of College Teaching." *Improving College and University Teaching,* 1980, *28,* 147–154.
French-Lazovik, G. "Predictability of Students' Evaluations of College Teachers from Component Ratings." *Journal of Educational Psychology,* 1974, *66,* 373–385.
French-Lazovik, G. *Evaluation of College Teaching: Guidelines for Summative and Formative Procedures.* Washington, D.C.: Association of American Colleges, 1976.
French-Lazovik, G. "Peer Review: Documentary Evidence in the Evaluation of Teaching." In Millman, J. (Ed.), *Handbook of Teacher Evaluation.* Beverly Hills, Calif.: Sage, 1981.
Guthrie, E. R. *The Evaluation of Teaching: A Progress Report.* Seattle: University of Washington, 1954.
O'Connell, W. R., and Smartt, S. H. *Improving Faculty Evaluation: A Trial in Strategy.* Atlanta, Ga.: Southern Regional Education Board, 1979.
Scriven, M. "The Methodology of Evaluation." *Perspectives of Curriculum Evaluation,* no. 1. American Educational Research Monograph Series, 1967.

Grace French-Lazovik is director of the Office for the Evaluation of Teaching at the University of Pittsburgh. Her work in teaching evaluation began over thirty years ago at the University of Washington with Professor Edwin Guthrie, one of the field's earliest pioneers.

The distinction between "direct" and "indirect" contributions is important for evaluation. A thorough appraisal of a faculty member's contribution to instruction requires an examination of both.

Using Colleague Ratings to Evaluate the Faculty Member's Contribution to Instruction

Donald P. Hoyt

The forces that mandate faculty evaluation are not likely to go away very quickly, so the debate is no longer about *whether* to evaluate but rather *how* to evaluate. Satisfying answers must be responsive both to the complexity of the problem and to the mischief that insensitive proposals can create.

In considering colleague ratings as a source of evaluative data, this chapter focuses exclusively on the faculty member's role as "instructor." Responsibilities in the research/creative realm and recognition for service to the public, profession, or institution, or for administration are specifically excluded in this discussion.

Further, because the research literature on this topic has been reviewed recently and well (Centra, 1979; Cohen and McKeachie, 1980; French-Lazovik, 1981), it would be redundant to refer to this work. Rather, this chapter focuses on the rationale for considering colleague ratings, the obstacles that impede their use, and the principles by which

G. French-Lazovik (Ed.). *New Directions for Teaching and Learning: Practices that Improve Teaching Evaluation*, no. 11. San Francisco: Jossey-Bass, September 1982.

they can make a constructive contribution to the evaluation of instructional effectiveness.

The Meaning of "Instructional Contribution"

When the educational process succeeds, important changes occur in the learner. Some of these changes can be observed over a brief period of time; others may require years before they manifest themselves. Useful ways to conceptualize these changes have been developed (Bloom and others, 1956; Krathwohl and others, 1964), so that it is common to focus on the cognitive, affective, and motor domains in describing learning objectives.

The purpose of education is to establish conditions that promote the individual's sense of fulfillment. This purpose implies not only the development of the individual's intellectual and motor capacities but also the discovery and elaboration of values and attitudes that direct and give meaning to his or her choices.

There are a variety of contributors to this purpose. College students learn much from roommates and friends. Life's unplanned experiences have been potent sources of learning, whether these occur in the workplace, the family, or the local tavern. The reading we choose to do, the commitment we make to developing our own faith, the neighbors we encounter at home and work are all important in determining how we develop and what meaning we find in life.

Against this framework, the role of the college teacher may seem unimportant. Indeed, some romanticized versions have exaggerated its influence. But it is a factor, and potentially an important one, in the developmental process we call learning.

There are two principal means by which a faculty member contributes to this process. In a direct way, the faculty member "teaches"— that is, informs. Whether by exposition, example, illustration, or other technique, the instructor provides the ingredients needed for learning and establishes the conditions that enhance receptivity on the part of the learner. There are potentially a number of indirect contributions also. These occur outside the hours for scheduled instruction and range from the tangible (the construction of instructional materials and plans, for instance), to the intangible (the creation of an environment that encourages and facilitates learning).

The distinction between "direct" and "indirect" contributions is important for evaluation. A thorough appraisal of a faculty member's contribution to instruction will require an examination of both. Therefore, evaluation systems should provide for collecting both types of information.

In general, research on the learning process supports the preceding generalizations. On the other hand, much is not yet known or understood. This is due in large part to our inability to assess human development on any but its simplest dimensions. Complex types of development (problem-solving skills, creativity, judgment, maturity, values) can currently be assessed only in relatively superficial and limited ways. These limitations in measurement are largely responsible for the ambiguities and uncertainties that characterize our current understanding of the learning process and that require us to proceed on the basis of assumptions rather than established fact.

Disagreements about procedures or methods usually are symptomatic of more fundamental disagreements about assumptions. It therefore seems prudent to identify one's assumptions at the start. This chapter assumes that learning is facilitated under three conditions: (1) objectives are established to direct learning activities and strategies; (2) experiences are provided that both stimulate activity on the part of the learner and provide access to the substantive material to be learned; and (3) feedback is provided that reinforces successful activity (activity that results in the desired learning) and redirects activity that is unsuccessful.

It is also assumed that the degree to which these conditions are established is only partially related to the way the instructor conducts the course. Students bring with them backgrounds, expectations, and motivations that have a telling effect on the amount and kind of learning that will occur. These student characteristics, in turn, can be influenced by a general atmosphere created by the faculty and other members of the learning community.

Finally, it is assumed that certain types of learning require more time and experience than any single course could provide. Generalized intellectual skills, such as problem solving, and self-understanding (including the development of and commitment to a system of personal values) represent fundamental purposes of higher education whose achievement requires lengthy experience. Such student development usually depends upon contributions from a large number of faculty members, and this leads some teachers to shun personal responsibility for facilitating it.

These assumptions suggest, then, that the instructional contribution of the faculty member has several facets. It is, indeed, concerned with the success with which the faculty member promotes learning in the classroom. But it is also concerned with facilitating learning in indirect ways. In particular, the faculty member influences (1) the degree to which good morale, teamwork, and cooperativeness exist in the department and the institution; (2) the development of curricula and courses that define a strategy for promoting learning; (3) the instructional skills and attitudes of other faculty members in the department or institution; and (4) the degree to which an atmosphere that supports and facilitates student learning is a major priority in the department and the institution.

The faculty member who has a positive effect on these matters makes a contribution to learning that would be totally overlooked if our framework for viewing contributions was restricted to classroom activity.

Colleague Qualifications as Evaluators

If colleagues are to play a role in faculty evaluation, it is necessary to establish that they have the opportunity to make relevant observations and that they are qualified to interpret those observations in a valid manner. There are, no doubt, situations where one or both of these conditions do not exist. Obviously, no rationale for using colleagues to assist in instructional evaluation can be made in such situations.

In typical departments, however, considerable opportunity for making relevant observations does exist. The most common formal mechanisms include departmental meetings, committee meetings, or team-teaching experiences. Informal opportunities occur through coffee breaks and spontaneous exchanges. While no one faculty member is able to observe all relevant activities of a colleague, the pooling of observations should improve comprehensiveness. From observations of these types, colleagues form impressions of the indirect contribution the individual makes to learning through assisting other faculty, contributing to curricula and course development, and establishing a positive and supportive learning environment.

Are colleagues qualified to judge such matters? Since typically the entire faculty must approve course and curricular changes, precedent suggests that they are competent to act in this area. Their experience as teachers qualifies them to judge the value of suggestions or other assistance offered by the faculty member to them or to colleagues. Contributions to the learning environment may appear more nebulous; but in most academic environments, faculty exhibit considerable consensus in identifying at least those whose contributions are at the extremes.

The instructor's direct contributions to learning cannot be validly judged by colleagues without structured assistance. To ask a faculty member to rate a colleague's classroom effectiveness on the basis of general observation would be inane; most such observations will be irrelevant to this characteristic. To require classroom visits as the basis for such ratings would be unrealistic (in terms of the time involved), potentially damaging to the spirit of colleagueship, and repetitious of information available from student ratings. A more reasonable position is to seek ratings of such key course management decisions as "selection of objectives," "reading assignments and other learning activities," and "appraisal of student progress." By reviewing instructional materials prepared by the faculty member (for example, a statement of objectives, a course outline, course assignments, examinations), colleagues who share the instructor's academic background should be able to judge the potential of such materials for contributing directly to student learning. Of course, the reliability and validity of such judgments can usually be improved if rating scales with carefully defined points are used.

Essentials of Effective Assessment

Books have been written on evaluation principles and their implications for evaluation processes (Williams, 1972; Anstey and others, 1976; Bolar, 1978). From this literature, we describe here those principles that experience has shown to be essential. Most of these principles address multiple concerns but, for convenience, have been organized around three criteria for a sound evaluation system, namely that procedures be credible, valid, and fair.

Regrettably, these characteristics are not always compatible. Therefore, actions taken to maximize one may detract from another. Practical considerations suggest that credibility is the most vital; the concerned parties must have confidence that the procedures are appropriate and will yield meaningful results. Credibility is largely a political matter. Without a dependable base of political support, few programs can succeed.

Validity, on the other hand, is primarily a technical concern. It refers to the comprehensiveness or completeness of evaluation processes and to the accuracy of the judgments that result from them. While it would be unethical to employ procedures or tools known to be invalid, it may be necessary to choose the less valid of two procedures in order to improve credibility.

The final criterion of sound evaluation systems is that they be fair. In contrast to the political nature of credibility and the technical nature of validity, fairness represents a moral imperative. It insists that professional ethics be followed, that procedures be applied uniformly, and that objectivity be pursued.

There are several principles of evaluation that emerge from these criteria.

Generalized Principles. Two principles are so fundamental that they support all three of the requirements of a sound evaluation program. These are the principle of *uniqueness* and the principle of *contextual interpretation.*

Uniqueness. The principle acknowledges that the foci for professional efforts necessarily differ significantly among positions which have the same title and job description. Idiosyncracies produced by history, present circumstances, and the local cast of characters will dictate that a unique set of expectations be established for each faculty member. Evalua-

62

tion, then, must focus on accomplishments relevant to these expectations; it is inappropriate to criticize or downgrade a faculty member for inattention to activities not included among the year's priorities.

Contextual Interpretation. When "student ahievement" is used to judge teaching effectiveness, those whose classes are dominated by highly motivated, intellectually quick students have an unfair advantage over those whose students are slow and resistant to learning. An effective evaluation system will take into account these considerations as well as other factors that may be beyond the individual's control (physical facilities for instruction, opportunity for the faculty member to prepare for the class, magnitude of the individual's total responsibilities, the opportunity to control major course features such as text or examinations, and so on).

Principles Related to Fairness. Activities and enterprises that lack a sound moral base have destructive tendencies that ultimately result in their own demise. Therefore, it is appropriate to begin with a review of principles specifically related to fairness. Besides the generalized principles noted above, fairness requires openness and relevance.

Openness. College or university evaluation procedures are not the place for hidden cameras, no matter how much they might contribute to validity. Those asked to report their observations or to make evaluative judgments should be told why their reactions are being sought, what will be done with their input, and what the rules are governing the confidentiality of their reports. Similarly, the process should not be mysterious to the person being evaluated.

Relevance. It would be unfair to fault a teacher of the retarded because none of his or her graduates had qualified as a Rhodes scholar. Similarly, it would be unfair to fault a faculty member for high costs per credit hour or declining course enrollments if his or her assignments were exclusively in areas unrelated to these disasters. Evaluative measures should bear a clear association to the responsibilities assigned to and accepted by the individual.

Principles Related to Credibility. Two additional principles of evaluation are especially useful for ensuring credibility. These are the principles of power and of reinforcement.

Power. The power principle states that, to be credible, evaluation procedures should be developed with input from all parties concerned. One reason that highly similar student evaluation systems have "originated" on hundreds of different campuses is the need for those affected to have their say; otherwise, the procedures will always be regarded as insensitive to the local situation. Sometimes, it *is* necessary to reinvent the wheel.

While the group or the individuals being evaluated clearly are entitled to provide advice, they are not the only interested parties. This is particularly true of faculty members whose work is of concern to students, colleagues, and superiors including the department head or chairperson. An evaluation system that denies any of these constituencies an opportunity to reveal their biases runs a serious credibility risk.

The principle does not require that all advice be accepted. It does require that opinions be sought, and that a rationale be formulated that shows that the system originators were aware of the perspective of each group.

Reinforcement. The second principle related to credibility is that of reinforcement. It states that the acceptability of evaluation procedures is a function of their potential for positive effects.

This principle is derived from the obvious fact that evaluation is inherently threatening. People have been programmed to focus on its negative effects, partly because, whenever a shakeup is desired, it is traditional to call for an evaluative review. More fundamentally, evaluation is a judgmental process; the *worth* of a person is presumably being determined. For the rare person whose high ego strength and self-confidence are justified by competence and accomplishment, evaluation may be a neutral, or even welcome, activity. But for the vast majority who harbor some self-doubts, who are aware of some personal weaknesses, and who desire and need the support and confidence of others, evaluation poses the distinct possibility that they'll be "found out."

Therefore, the evaluation sytsem should feature the potential for gain. That is, if it discovers something amiss, it should provide some mechanism for righting it. This may mean "improving instructional skills"; it may also mean increasing resources, altering priorities, or reorganizing work schedules.

Principles Related to Validity. Two components determine the validity of evaluations—comprehensiveness and accuracy. Principles related to validity, other than the generalized principles, stress one or the other of these components.

Criterion Specification. One of the major mistakes made by evaluation neophytes is the confusion of "description" with "evaluation." A description of activities is different from a judgment of their impact. It is much more important to know what happened as a result of the instructor's activities than whether he or she worked hard, was on time, or called people by their first names.

The principle requires that, for each of the major activities identified by the position description, relevant outcomes be described. Valid evaluation procedures will specify the changes (in people, situations, or accomplishments) that differentiate the successful from the unsuccessful. The process of identifying relevant criteria will also require specifying appropriate time frames. Some outcomes will be observable only after several years, while others are relatively continuous.

As noted earlier, many of the most important outcomes of instruction cannot yet be assessed accurately. Rather than ignore such outcomes, many evaluators develop proxy measures. This requires the assessment of activities or products that are assumed to contribute to the outcomes in question.

Face Value of Evidence. A second principle related to validity requires that evidence used for appraisal have face validity. There should be no dispute as to the relevance of each piece of evaluative information.

Many systems that relied on student ratings of instruction to evaluate teaching effectiveness have failed because they asked students to make judgments for which they were unqualified (such as, did the teacher know the material?) or asked for ratings of characteristics whose relevance to teaching effectiveness was dubious (such as the teacher's sense of humor). Although there are probably many indicators of effectiveness in instruction, the number that have been validated by consensus or by research is quite limited. It is better to restrict evaluations to validated indicators than to seek comprehensiveness by including characteristics whose relevance is neither established nor accepted.

Representative Input. One of the most serious affronts to the dignity of a "true-blue" evaluator is a system that depends on the input of those who are clearly unrepresentative. Letters of recommendation, office calls from one or two disgruntled students, and washroom complaints from one or two colleagues share this characteristic. Little can be learned from such unrepresentative sources, even if honesty could be assured.

Given the shaky reliability and validity of the observations of any one individual, it is vital to ensure that judgments from a given source are representative of that source. In the case of colleague ratings, some compromise is required between this goal and the desirability of minimizing the time and effort the system requires.

Implications. Although a fundamental assertion of this chapter is that colleagues can be a useful source of evaluative information, the credibility criterion requires the acknowledgment that, if the faculty members object to a plan requiring such ratings, a new plan should be prepared. Some of the reasons for faculty resistance are reviewed in the next section.

In situations where faculty members are willing to consider colleague ratings as an element of teaching evaluation, three arguments usually prevail: (1) students are ill-equipped to make judgments about several critically important factors—as a consequence, "superficial showmen" or "entertainers" typically receive a favorable reception from students; (2) it is impractical to obtain reports from previous students about the long-term, enduring impact of the teacher, even though such effects are much more important than the immediate outcomes that students typically use to rate their teachers; (3) many faculty members make major contributions to student learning by indirect means (such as curriculum development or the fostering of faculty development), which students have no opportunity to observe.

When it has been determined that colleague ratings will constitute an element in the plan for evaluating instructional effectiveness, it is desirable that the principles described in this section be followed as closely as possible. Thus, the faculty members themselves should be principally responsible for designing the procedures. Differences among teaching assignments should be recognized, so that no faculty member is being judged by standards or criteria that are irrelavant, or only tangentially relevant, to the courses, objectives, and students that are her or his responsibility. The process should produce something positive; typically, this means some constructive suggestions should be offered for enhancing the faculty member's effectiveness.

Colleagues should be asked to report or interpret only those activities that they have observed. Assumptions that relate each activity or rating to student growth should be explicit and should have general faculty endorsement. Policies describing the purposes of the ratings, their accessibility, and confidentiality should be clearly stated.

Issues and Controversies

Formal colleague ratings are not widely used as an important means of evaluating instructional effectiveness (Batista, 1976; Miller, 1972; Seldin, 1975). This is due in part to the lack of credible, valid, and fair methods for obtaining such ratings. But there are several other circumstances that help account for the general neglect of this source of evaluative information.

Faculty Resistance. While faculty members appear to agree that ratings of current students are inadequate for the comprehensive appraisal of instructional effectiveness, they commonly resist proposals to add colleague ratings. Aside from objections to the sizable time and effort requirements that colleague rating schemes require, there are several political or philosophical concerns. The most prominent of these include:

1. *Conflict of interest* argument: Faculty members dislike being placed in the position where their own welfare is influenced by what they say about their colleagues. Funds for salary increases in a given department are usually fixed; a high increase for a colleague, resulting from another's high ratings, reduces the potential financial rewards available to the rater.

2. The *conflict with colleagueship* argument: Intellectual and academic efforts are best achieved in an atmosphere of cooperation and mutual respect. To require faculty members to make evaluative judgments of each other creates suspicion, apprehension, and defensiveness that undermines such an atmosphere.

3. The *administrative copout* argument: Administrators seek faculty ratings of their colleagues as a way of avoiding their own responsibilities. By substituting "democracy" for "judgment," they scatter hostility while avoiding accountability.

4. The *evaluation trap* argument: This argument is used to resist faculty evaluation by any means, not just by colleagues. It assumes that the academic and intellectual purposes of higher education require maximum freedom and flexibility for the faculty. Since evaluation schemes state or imply specific, but limited, objectives, they require the faculty member to direct attention to predetermined goals, and they detract from the spontaneity and creativity that are essential to effective functioning.

These arguments must be juxtaposed with those describing the advantages of expanding the evaluative base. In situations where feelings run strong, more may be lost than gained by requiring a colleague rating system. In addition to such irrational factors as personal bias, suspicion, and conspiracy, the degree to which colleague ratings have credibility and validity for the faculty will depend on the specific procedures proposed. Unless there is a full opportunity for faculty to consider a thoughtful and sensitive proposal, it will be difficult to judge the acceptability of colleague ratings.

Selecting Faculty Raters. The task of judging the effectiveness of colleagues is both onerous and demanding. Procedures should be chosen that minimize the effort required as well as the prospects of creating schisms among faculty. One principle is to share the responsibility by using several raters. A second is to keep the number of raters to a minimum in the interest of efficiency.

The problem in selecting raters is twofold. Each rater is fallible, so provision must be made for minimizing judgmental errors. And no rater has had a full opportunity to observe, so provision must be made to ensure that ratings reflect comprehensively the faculty member's functioning.

Indirect contributions to the instructional program are made through day-to-day activities that can be observed by all faculty members in the department. Therefore, it is appropriate to seek the views of the entire departmental faculty on these matters. The means for reporting these views should be made as simple and efficient as possible.

To make sound evaluative judgments or an individual's direct contributions will require more care and effort. Experience suggests that, if the rating task is properly structured and if appropriate standard materials are presented as the basis for rating, satisfactory reliability can be obtained by using three independent raters.

Two alternatives exist for selecting these raters. In the first, each faculty member identifies all colleagues who have had sufficient opportunity to observe the professional performance in question (that is, instruction, research, and so on). From this roster, three raters are drawn at random and asked to make ratings on a standard scale. Ratings are made independently and anonymously.

The second alternative asks each faculty member to provide a standard set of materials that will form the basis for colleague ratings. Although three raters could be selected randomly to provide independent ratings for each faculty member, it is generally more satisfactory to have the faculty elect a team of three. Separate teams are usually elected for rating instructional, research, and service responsibilities. Rules that limit the number of times a given individual is eligible for election to a team provide necessary safeguards against the long-term effects of personal biases and also protect faculty raters from an unreasonable amount of involvement in evaluation.

Due Process and Anonymity. Considerable evidence exists to conclude that ratings obtained under conditions of anonymity differ significantly from those that are publicly attributed to individuals (Kane and Lawler, 1978; Landy and Farr, 1980). It is generally believed that the more generous ratings received when the judgments of specific raters are made known reflects a natural reluctance to invite the ill will of those being evaluated. While anonymity seems to invite irresponsibility and offer protection to those wishing to settle old scores, the use of multiple raters diminishes this threat. Interestingly, evidence to date suggests that ratings collected under "anonymous" and "identified" conditions are about equal in validity, even though they differ significantly in both level and variability.

Faculty members are sometimes suspicious that the administrator who synthesizes all evaluative information, including that from colleague ratings, uses the protection of rater anonymity to distort the synthesis. A claim that colleague ratings were low can't be disputed if the anonymity agreement makes confirmation impossible. Therefore, a mechanism that permits independent verification of these ratings should be established.

Recent court rulings as to whether or not confidentiality can be protected from legal challenge are contradictory. (See Blaubergs versus Regents of the University System of Georgia and Gray versus Board of Higher Education as reported in the *United States Law Week*, 1981.) If disputes have gone that far, it seems unlikely that friendships and collegiality will be restored, with or without confidentiality.

Conclusions and Recommendations

The conditions that make colleague ratings a potentially valuable feature of an instructional evaluation system are:

1. General agreement that evaluation is an important and potentially valuable activity

2. General agreement that instruction is sufficiently important that its evaluation merits serious attention and effort

3. General agreement that there are other faculty members who are capable of making valid assessments of instructional contributions that students are not qualified to assess

4. A proposal that avoids making unreasonable demands on the time and effort required for implementation

5. A proposal that emphasizes constructive features

Clearly, if the faculty in a decision-making unit (department, division, or college) reaches a consensus on the first three of these, a prudent next step is to charge a small group with developing one or more proposals for the faculty's later consideration.

The use of colleague ratings to evaluate instructional effectiveness is contraindicated by the absence of these five conditions. It may also be wise to discard or postpone such proposals if one or two faculty members are so adamantly opposed that they threaten legal action while the remaining members of the faculty have no strong views on the matter. Under such circumstances, more will probably be lost than gained by implementing the proposal.

Minimize Required Effort. A common mistake of those developing evaluation systems is to make them too elaborate and comprehensive. For judging indirect contributions, a simple but workable illustration is given below. The content and description of "indirect contributions" will vary from institution to institution and even among departments in the same institution, so that no standard form can be prescribed. Simplicity and efficiency, however, should characterize whatever means are used to appraise indirect contributions.

Similarly, evaluation of every course every term will ensure the early demise of a system for judging direct contributions. Of course, it is important to review all instructional responsibilities, but not all at once. The system might require, for example, that the faculty member and department chairman come to an agreement on, say, three classes that will be evaluated during a given year; the only constraint on the choice of classes is that each of the individual's instructional assignments must be reviewed at least once over a three-year period. This not only reduces the effort required but also allows the individual to concentrate improvement efforts rather than dissipate them across the entire schedule of classes.

Care should also be taken to collect only the most relevant information. A system that asks faculty members to supply raters with "materials descriptive of your instruction," or that asks colleagues to wade through the mountains of paper that such a mandate would produce (at least from the more insecure members of the faculty), will create unreasonable and unnecessary effort for both raters and faculty. The undesirability of classroom visitations has been mentioned previously. Ideally, the system

Directions

Part of the system for evaluating instructional effectiveness requires the gathering of relevant faculty observations of their colleagues. Your ratings will be used by the department head in arriving at an overall evaluation. Individual faculty members will be provided a summary of colleague ratings, but the ratings by individual faculty members will be considered confidential.

1. Draw a line through your own name.
2. On the basis of your observations over the past 12 months, rate the other faculty members on each of the three types of contributions described below. Use the following code:

> ? = Insufficient opportunity to observe
> - = Contribution was negative
> 0 = Neither a negative nor positive contribution
> + = Contribution was generally positive
> ++ = Contribution was extremely positive

	COLUMN 1 Environment	COLUMN 2 Course,Curricular	COLUMN 3 Assisting Faculty
Faculty Member 1	____	____	____
Faculty Member 2	____	____	____
.	.	.	.
.	.	.	.
Faculty Member N	____	____	____

DESCRIPTION OF THE CHARACTERISTICS TO BE RATED

Column 1. Contributions to a positive learning environment. Expresses interest in the academic work of others. Shares with others his/her own ideas, hypotheses, projects, etc. By demeanor and example, encourages curiosity and inquiry. Models intellectual ideals (openness, carefulness, integrity, broad interests, objectivity, tolerance of ambiguity, etc.).

Column 2. Contributions to course and curricular development. Refines and updates courses. Develops new instructional materials and/or learning aids. Calls the faculty's attention to instructional or curricular innovations which have been tried elsewhere. Discusses ways to improve integration and articulation of his/her courses with those of other faculty. Initiates and/or contributes to discussions of desirable curriculum changes.

Column 3. Contributions to teaching effectiveness of others. Is consulted by other faculty on instructional matters. Gives teaching assistants advice on teaching. Suggests ways for faculty or assistants to improve classroom or examination procedures. Invites colleagues to visit his/her classes and discuss strategy and tactics. Accepts invitations to visit and critique colleagues' instruction.

should focus on a few credible concepts that students are not qualified to rate and for which most faculty members can supply relevant material. Information about instructional objectives, readings and/or other assignments, and examinations has considerable credibility for judging direct instructional contributions.

Maximize Formative Benefits. Develop ways for recording evaluative observations that offer constructive assistance. This is especially important in evaluating direct contributions.

As an illustration, consider the element of "instructional objecctives." Assume the instructor has submitted a list of objectives for a particular course. At the grossest level, colleagues might be asked to rate the objectives on a five-point scale ranging from "1 = definite weakness" to "5 = definite strength". At a more refined level, several general characteristics of objectives might be identified—such as clarity, appropriateness, and comprehensiveness—and each rated on a scale from "1 = needs improvement" to "5 = outstanding". While this approach is more helpful in identifying a starting place for improvement, it is less explicit than the following example:

> *Objectives.* Overall, what effect do you believe the statement of objectives had on promoting student learning in this course?
> __ Highly positive __ Positive __ No effect __ Negative
> Identify specific objectives that appear to be:
> a) Overemphasized _____
> b) Overly ambitious _____
> c) Lacking in challenge _____
> d) Underemphasized or neglected _____
>   (include omissions) _____
> e) Ambiguous _____

A format like this provides the necessary summative judgment, but it also adds specific guidance for improvement efforts. In addition, it encourages raters to give the task thoughtful and professional attention.

Avoid Norm Referencing. Rating forms that contain words like "average," "below average," or "above average" predictably will create more costs than benefits. Perhaps more than most segments of society, faculty members are afflicted with the sin of pride. The route that each traveled to attain his or her present status was filled with academic challenges. Characteristically, the faculty member met these challenges successfully; he or she "won." Each message along the way confirmed the individual's "exceptionality" (and possibly added to deficiencies in humility). The most obvious feature of a norm-based evaluation is that half of these outstanding "winners" is below average. Such bad news is not likely to engender faculty enthusiasm.

Ratings should describe the effect, or probable effect, of a particular effort. The scale should reflect the degree to which a desired outcome was achieved, not how this compared with the efforts of other faculty members. If all faculty members develop sound objectives and use them effectively to promote learning, the ratings should reflect this rather than arbitrarily inflict "below average" ratings on half the group.

Maintain Perspective. Faculty evaluation programs create a need for perspective both from the frame of reference of the task itself and from the frame of reference of the individual.

With respect to the task, it is important to stress two characteristics of the evaluation program. First, it has a definite formative dimension. The institution, the department, and its chairperson or head should make it clear to all that an attempt will be made to diagnose professional strengths and weaknesses and that assistance will be offered to foster faculty development. Faculty members should not find their positions jeopardized by professional shortcomings of which they have never been advised. Second, the major summative decisions are made on the basis of comprehensive, long-term evaluation evidence. Evaluation systems should make it clear that all aspects of faculty performance will be considered and that efforts will be made to take into account the effects of faculty development activities initiated on the basis of previous evaluations. The system and process should be one that results in very few surprises when promotion and tenure decisions are made.

To the individual faculty member, evaluation threatens self-esteem. Increasingly, however, there is consensual acknowledgment of its necessity. It is imperative that means be found for minimizing disruptions due to this threat. Emphasizing formative purposes has already been suggested. Beyond that, advantage should be taken of opportunities that remind faculty members of the intrinsic rewards of their profession. The evaluation process inevitably focuses on the judgments of others and, in the summative mode, creates a tie between these judgments and externally administered rewards (such as salary, promotion, or tenure). But no external authority can supply the satisfactions available from intellectual give-and-take, from advising and guiding young people in choosing directions for their life, from the unending discovery of ideas, facts, and creative expressions, or from the stimulation of another's mind and heart. Care must be taken to preserve, encourage, and emphasize these internally administered satisfactions. Otherwise, there is danger that evaluation's focus on the judgments of others will fix the faculty's attention on a reward process that is externally administered and controlled (Deci, 1975; Lepper and Greene, 1975). No matter how elegant the resulting evaluations, much mischief has been done if the joys of teaching are diminished.

72

References

Anstey, E., Fletcher, C., and Walker, J. *Staff Appraisal and Development*. London: Allen & Unwin, 1976.

Batista, E. E. "The Place of Colleague Evaluation in the Appraisal of College Teaching: A Review of the Literature." *Research in Higher Education*, 1976, *4*, 157–271.

Bloom, B. S., Englebart, M. D., Furst, E. J., Hill, W. H., and Krathwohl, D. R. *A Taxonomy of Educational Objectives: Handbook I, The Cognitive Domain*. New York: Longman, 1956.

Bolar, M. (Ed.). *Performance Appraisal: Readings, Case Studies, and Survey of Practices*. New Delhi: Vikas, 1978.

Centra, J. A. "Evaluation of Colleagues." In Centra, J. A., *Determining Faculty Effectiveness*. San Francisco: Jossey-Bass, 1979.

Cohen, P. A., and McKeachie, W. J. "The Role of Colleagues in the Evaluation of College Teaching." *Improving College and University Teaching*, 1980, *28*, 147–154.

Deci, E. L. *Intrinsic Motivation*. New York: Plenum, 1975.

French-Lazovik, G. "Peer Review: Documentary Evidence in the Evaluation of Teaching." In J. Millman (Ed.), *Handbook of Teacher Evaluation*. Beverly Hills, Calif.: Sage, 1981.

Kane, J. S., and Lawler, E. F., III. "Methods of Peer Assessment." *Psychological Bulletin*, 1978, *85*, 555–586.

Krathwohl, D. R., Bloom, B. S., and Masia, B. *A Taxonomy of Educational Objectives: Handbook II, The Affective Domain*. New York: MacKay, 1964.

Landy, F. J., and Farr, J. L. "Performance Rating." *Psychological Bulletin*, 1980, *87*, 72–107.

Lepper, M. R., and Greene, D. "Turning Play into Work: Effects of Adult Surveillance and Extrinsic Rewards on Children's Intrinsic Motivation." *Journal of Personality and Social Psychology*, 1975, *31*, 479–486.

Miller, R. I. *Evaluating Faculty Performance*. San Francisco: Jossey-Bass, 1972.

Seldin, P. *How Colleges Evaluate Professors*. New York: Blythe-Pennington, 1975.

United States Law Week. November 24, 1981, pp. 2306–2307.

Williams, M. R. *Performance Appraisal in Management*. London: Heinemann Educational Books, 1972.

*As assistant provost and director of educational resources
at Kansas State University, Donald P. Hoyt coordinates
faculty evaluation activities and has developed
widely used instruments for assessing teaching
and administrative performance.*

This chapter exposes weaknesses in current
evaluation practices, showing how subjective
judgments often subvert supposedly objective
procedures, and suggests a remedy.

Can Faculty Objectively
Evaluate Teaching?

Kenneth E. Eble

This chapter proceeds from what I take to be a current description of
faculty evaluation: essentially a pluralistic, multilayered system that
attempts to be objective but in which highly subjective opinion plays a
prominent part (Gustad, 1961; Southern Regional Education Board,
1977). The criteria for retention, promotion, and tenure decisions rest on
that convenient if shaky metaphor, the three-legged stool of research,
teaching, and service.

The first and most important level of recommendation is the
judgment of faculty peers carried out through data gathering, examining,
discussing, and voting by department or division colleagues. Though the
structure varies somewhat with the size of institution, most institutions
have one or more levels of review, from dean to academic vice-president
and from college personnel committees to university-wide review and
grievance bodies. In most systems, final authority rests with the president
or trustees, though concurrence with lower-level recommendations is
clearly the prevailing practice. Also in most systems, faculty members are
heavily involved, and administrative decision-making power is demonstrated only enough to create some degree of tension between faculty and
administration.

G. French-Lazovik (Ed.). *New Directions for Teaching and Learning:*
Practices that Improve Teaching Evaluation, no. 11. San Francisco: Jossey-Bass, September 1982.

Within the system, faculty productivity, usually defined as research publication or the equivalent, is the dominant value, despite the fact that within any faculty at any time, the majority of members are not engaging in substantial publishable work. Teaching commonly "weighs" less than research and more than service, but few institutions deny the importance of teaching and, in most, modest achievements in teaching are tolerated fully as much as are modest achievements in research.

Faculty Attitudes Toward Teaching, Research, and Service

To focus on "peer evaluation of teaching," as does this chapter, is limiting and artificial, for "peer evaluation" is only one aspect, albeit the most important aspect, of an evaluation system, and teaching is only one aspect of faculty performance. Much of what I write applies as fully to other aspects of faculty service and its measurement as it does to teaching. Moreover, discussing improvements in evaluating teaching brings up questions about the values both individuals and institutions hold and how these values get translated into the means by which other services are evaluated.

Faculty members themselves have conflicting attitudes about the values they and their institutions place upon the various services expected of faculty. A sizable portion of the faculty—particularly in the sciences— feels its highest duty is to research, however these faculty members harmonize or do not harmonize research with teaching. An equally sizable portion, probably the majority of all faculty if all institutions are taken into account, regards teaching as its most important duty, though many of these faculty members will measure their worth by their achievements or lack of achievements in scholarship.

A recent report of the task force on teaching evaluation at the University of California, Berkeley (Wilson and others, 1980), gives some precise information about these attitudes. When faculty were asked to indicate, on a scale of 100, what they thought was the emphasis placed upon teaching, research and creative work, professional competence, and service, they indicated 20 for teaching, 57 for research and creative work, 13 for professional competence, and 9 for service. When asked what they thought the emphasis *should be,* they responded with 31 for teaching, 43 for research and creative work, 16 for professional competence, and 11 for service.

A slightly different survey at the University of Michigan (Ericksen, 1978) drew similar responses. Asked "what is the relative weight given to research, teaching, and service for promotion in your department?" faculty responded: 64 for research, 26 for teaching, and 10 for service. As at the University of California, research is perceived to be something more than twice as important as teaching, despite the fact that assistant professors said they gave 48 percent of their time to teaching against 32 percent to research and that teaching provided more satisfaction (47 percent) than research (38 percent).

At Berkeley, assistant professors and associates disagreed sharply with chairpersons and full professors over the question, "Was the system fair and equitable to teaching?" Seventy percent of chairpersons and 55 percent of full professors found it fair and equitable as against 27 percent of assistant professors and 40 percent of associates. At Michigan the interviewers wrote: "From our interviews it is clear that the pressure to be productive as a researcher/scholar is internal as well as external and reflects a faculty member's own conception of the aim of a research-oriented university such as this one . . . Again and again, however, faculty members express the view that the rewards for good teaching are lacking here at the University. They consistently complained that teaching is not rewarded to the extent that research is." At Berkeley, the report identified the two primary sources of dissatisfaction with the current review process as "(1) the relative emphasis given to teaching and (2) the nature and quality of evidence used to make judgments about the quality of a faculty member's teaching" (p. 81).

Pecularities of Evaluating Teaching

To assist in placing the focus on teaching but without isolating it from the other duties by which faculty are measured, let me suggest some particular characteristics that apply to evaluating teaching. First, the evaluation of teaching is felt by many faculty members to be a more personal measurement than that made of their other services. Although some faculty members may be merely shielding their deficiencies by resisting any direct evaluation of teaching, more probably resist because they ascertain that a judgment is being placed on them personally. Research, by its nature, is detached from the individual, and though it stings, personally, to have a grant proposal rejected or one's research go unrecognized, the hurt is not as personal as arises from criticism of one's teaching.

Second, research tends to receive its most significant evaluations at a distance from one's colleagues. However colleagues may be involved in passing judgment on what one has produced, production in itself carries a large amount of credibility. Further, the rejection or acceptance of a manuscript is not often by department colleagues. Most often, the proposals for research and the results of research are judged by unidentified and at-a-distance referees. Those who make adverse decisions may have done so from bad motives and low intelligence, but they are not supposed friends and near acquaintances.

Third, with but few exceptions, teaching has no quantitative measures as definite, for example, as the counting of publications. Everyone teaches in fairly equitable amounts; the quantitative records of professors in the same rank with respect to teaching would show much less difference than the quantitative records for publication or service. Moreover, there is little sophistication in examining *what* a person teaches, how many students are being taught, and what declines or advances may be evidenced.

Fourth, qualitative measures for teaching are very hard to obtain and are not likely to have a roughly comparable level of acceptance among faculty. Measuring the quality of research presents similar difficulties, but the acceptance by faculty of the rough measures that we do have is much higher than for teaching.

If I am right in my speculations about the pecularities attached to evaluating teaching, these help explain why this type of evaluating has proceeded cautiously and amidst fears, anxieties, and hostility.

Nevertheless, during the past decade, a majority of faculty have accepted more searching evaluations of teaching (Centra, 1979; Seldin, 1980). The use of formal student evaluations has been the most conspicuous increase in the ways by which institutions try to measure teaching competence. A familiar reaction of faculty facing a formalized student evaluation—that it can be used for improvement but not for retention, promotion, and tenure decisions—has given way to a recognition that student evaluations can serve both purposes. Perhaps the acceptance of student evaluation, as well as acceptance of more searching evaluation practices of other kinds, is based on the fact that faculties still retain the basic right of peer review. They can, therefore, see that student evaluations are used properly or, to put it another way, they can easily subvert the evidence that student evaluations may provide.

The Right of Peer Review

The security provided by peer review, then, may account for the acceptance by faculty of more rigorous efforts to evaluate faculty services and, in particular, teaching. After all, faculty members create the climate in which an evaluation system works or does not work. This process is probably not clearly understood on any campus, nor is the faculty exclusively responsible. Strong presidents in autocratic institutions, along with strong deans or chairpersons, can make known what they value and even bring about schemes to measure it. The quality and kind of students can also have an impact on the willingness or unwillingness of faculty members to accept and use student evaluations. But however faculty may complain about administrative or student pressures, the pressures that arise within evaluation systems are self-pressures. Some kind of collective recognition by the faculty establishes the larger values by which individual efforts are measured. That collective recognition also includes the receptivity or rejection of certain kinds of evaluation—whether, for example, student input will be responsibly and judiciously used, or how much and what kind of faculty energy will be given to gathering and interpreting data. In the chronic arguments over "publish or perish," the fact is that the faculty both creates the pressure to publish in the abstract and then renders adverse judgments in particular instances.

The right of faculty to pass judgment on their colleagues has a long history and has been strengthened through the years by actions of professional associations and unions (Mason, 1972; Levenstein, 1977). Collective bargaining has affected the practice in some details but probably the factor that has had the greatest impact on peer review is the diminishing willingness of many faculty members in the last decade to be responsibly involved in academic governance. An uneasiness about secrecy in procedures has brought about more access to files and more concern about the defensibility of data. The stress on accountability and the research into evaluation of teaching have brought about improvements in peer review practices and greater sophistication and elaboration of data-collecting procedures. Yet these and other changes have not altered the basic fact that the crucial judgments in the reward system are those made by faculty colleagues, whatever the data and however they may be used.

Criticism of the System

Given reasonable guarantees of advancement, most faculty members, like most other human beings, would probably not choose to be evaluated. Faced with the necessity and an imperfect system largely of their own devising, faculties chronically criticize and try to improve the system. Four common sources of criticism are (1) the value system of the college and university as against those of the department or division; (2) the conflicts among various loyalties of faculty members to the department, the college, the discipline, the students, their own ideals, and others; (3) economic realities and pressures; (4) self-interest versus institutional or social interests.

Within both small colleges and very large universities, there are marked differences in values held by the institution at large and by the faculty working largely within department units (Gustad, 1960; Southern Regional Education Board, 1977). All institutions are affected by their public image, hence the continuing exploitation of college athletics as the most conspicuous means of advertising the institution's merits. All faculty are affected by an individual's standing in or relation to the disciplinary field in which he or she works. Institutional values will be pulled in the direction of the public image (a winning football team, for example) and, by analogy, of winners on the faculty (such as Nobel

Prize winning physicists). Faculty values will be pulled in the direction of disciplinary excellence, hence a partial explanation of departmental provincialism.

Moreover, departments themselves differ in the values they hold. With respect to teaching, there are very few awards that distinguish among faculty members beyond the range of their own colleges or universities. John Bevan, earlier in this volume, pointed out the general lack of incentives offered for "the encouragement, renewal, and development" of faculty members. Some departments are strongly research departments, with their faculty members (molecular biologists, for example) in the public eye. Other departments have a heavy burden (as it is generally regarded) of service functions, like the teaching of basic composition or mathematics, which go relatively unnoticed.

These and other differences in the values attached to various faculty services make the enunciation of overall values extremely difficult. In very large universities, even the large departments may have difficulty in reaching agreements as to the values that should underlie evaluation policies and practices. In the years ahead, the tight job market in many disciplines may bring about more friction between an institution's values and those of the departmental faculty. Faculty members who might have opted for a more research-oriented position in better times will probably accept positions in colleges oriented much more toward teaching and service. Some institutions will see the favorable job market as an opportunity to upgrade the faculty and this usually means a greater emphasis upon research, publication, and national recognition. Those institutions with long-established research missions and many other institutions striving toward that goal will probably continue to pay the customary lip-service to teaching, but as institutional values translate themselves into the reward system, those who primarily teach and teach very well may find lower-level recommendations turned back at the higher levels of review.

In the functioning of peer review (and setting aside all ignoble proclivities), faculty members gauge others by the measure of themselves. Where faculty vote is the determining judgment, the widely differing values held by the voters themselves reduce the fit between agreed-upon criteria and the decisions made on individual faculty members. I am not talking here about the effects of personal friendships and antagonisms but of the varying values that faculty attach to teaching, research, and service. Faculty members who see themselves primarily as teachers are likely to give more weight to the teaching excellence of other faculty members. If a faculty member hasn't published lately or ever, he or she is likely to excuse a similar lack of productivity in a colleague. In other words, these value differences create a looseness in the workings of the democratic vote.

Since there is some evidence that intrinsic rather than extrinsic rewards are more important to faculty (Gustad, 1960), economic realities and pressures may have less significance than the values that individuals and institutions hold. Nevertheless, the spread of collective bargaining in itself attests to the seriousness with which faculty contend for salary dollars. In financially hard times, exacerbations over evaluations will be intensified. Economic self-interest on the part of many faculty members may well diminish the value of teaching in peer review. For one thing, research accomplishments are the chief means of becoming competitive on a national market. Consultantships, grants, prizes, and commercial publications of various kinds are achieved more often through research than through teaching. With diminishing revenues from many sources, institutions already place a premium on those who can win outside money by obtaining research grants.

Finally, all evaluation systems arouse a conflict between the individual and the institution. The individual's basic self-interest is to keep his job; the institution's may be to find a better person to fill it. Only the facts that faculty are protected to some degree by the system of peer review and are conditioned to their institutional status keep grievances about evaluation decisions as few as they are. Short of grievances, the reward system has within it fundamental conflicts between how individuals perceive themselves and how they are perceived by their peers or their institution. As systems attempt to become more rigorous and even as they may succeed in improving performance, the benign acceptance of these conflicts may disappear.

Faculty Role and Responsibilities

Given such an imperfect system and the internal conflicts of its operation, what role should faculty play in effectively evaluating teaching? First, faculty responsibilities begin well before the discussing and voting that decides the fate of a colleague. Faculty members must be involved with enunciating, reviewing, and recasting, when necessary, the values that underlie evaluating at all vital levels: the department, the college, and the university at large. Faculty members must also work toward honest and usable statements of university expectations of the faculty. And, at the first level of review, faculty members must, apart from the specific reviewing of colleagues, thrash out what the collective values of the department are and how they can be specifically and concretely embodied in written policies and fair practices.

Second, faculty members must come forward to engage more often and more openly in discussions about the values they hold. The reading of scholarly papers to discretely knowing audiences, the attendance at professional meetings, the keeping of students at arm's length as regards their perspectives on teaching and learning, the occasional hearsay about the work of one's colleagues—these are obviously inadequate if faculty members would function as citizens reasonably prepared to cast their retention, promotion, and tenure votes. Too much of academic life is a preoccupation with one's own specialized work, a toleration for everything that does not directly impinge upon it, and a suspension of formal judgment (despite the presence of strong internal prejudices and convictions) about most matters that lie outside one's field of expertise.

Third, faculty members need to resist the dog-eat-dog financial conditions under which many faculties operate. In inflationary times, salary increases strictly on a merit basis cannot help but be demoralizing. Using student evaluations to arrive at faculty ratings of 1, 2, 3, or 4, to fix salary increases, and to decide upon promotions and tenure is a similarly ill-advised practice.

As to the faculty's specific responsibilities within the actual reward system, much depends upon the time and intelligence faculty members are willing to commit to it. As long as peer review remains a central principle, the faculty's sense of responsibility, active involvement, and collective judgment will affect the system crucially, however good or bad the system may be. At the minimum level of involvement, the faculty must be willing to gather data carefully, examine and weigh them judiciously, interact with colleagues to refine opinion and fill out the written record, and take on specific responsibilities necessary to the functioning of the system. At a maximum, faculty must do all these plus become informed about aspects of evaluating teaching and other services, become careful observers and critics of the effectiveness of the various processes in the system, acquaint themselves with the workings of the entire system, and contribute in appropriate ways to its effectiveness and improvement.

Reducing the Effects of Subjective Judgments

The most serious specific weakness in the current evaluation system is surely the subjective biases that operate so forcefully at the primary level of peer review. Department chairpersons, deans, and presidents also have their subjective biases, but almost always they can only be manifested against the collective biases of the faculty in the form of decisions already reached.

The system itself is not without some features that try to offset subjective judgments. The responsibility for gathering and interpreting valid data with which I have just charged the faculty has, as one aim, the introduction of more objective data into the procedures. Discussion and voting procedures serve to balance out individual subjectivity even though the result may be a collective subjective judgment. Independent recomendations of chairpersons, deans, and committees are another kind of mechanism for offsetting the subjective judgments of department peers. Student evaluation has entered into systems in part as a means of affording a judgment on teaching from another perspective than that of faculty. Outside referees of research and publications perform a similar function. The various guidelines, forms, and worksheets set forth in individual essays in this volume are other means of getting less subjective data.

The limiting characteristics of all these and other measures are the time that faculty members are willing to spend, the financial investment that the institution is willing to make, and the complexity that an effective system will sustain. When a faculty decides that time spent in evaluating is infringing upon time for teaching and research, when evaluation responsibilities are given lip-service but carried out poorly, when resentments about the time and trouble of evaluating cloud the judgments that result—these are clear signs that efforts to improve the system have become counterproductive. Any attempts to reduce the subjectivity of peer review must keep in mind the extent to which faculty will become responsibly involved or will turn part of their responsibility over to others.

Getting first-hand information about a colleague's teaching by the faculty is an obvious way of reducing the weight of subjective opinion, but it makes great demands on faculty members' time (Seldin, 1980). All attempts to observe teaching require extensive and careful visiting; the quality of the data to some degree depends on the extent of visiting, both in sampling a large number of classes and in obtaining the views of a considerable number of faculty. Trained observers using more precisely defined criteria may be superior to colleague visiting and save a department faculty's time, but the trained observer's time must be counted as a cost of evaluation. Few departments spend any part of their budgets for such services.

Because of these practical limitations on faculty visiting and because I think student evaluations afford better data (McKeachie, 1977), I think faculty time is best spent in maintaining a consistent and reliable student evaluation of teaching. No faculty visiting program can match the observations that students make, day after day, in all variety of classes. To supplement that information—but this *will* take faculty time—departments should routinely keep files of the tangible evidences of a faculty member's teaching: classes and level of classes, numbers of students, course outlines and syllabi, grading practices, tests and exercises, and the like (Knapper and others, 1977; French-Lazovik, 1981). The record-keeping aspect should be absorbed by an effectively administered department; the evaluating aspect once again makes demands on faculty members' time. Though I think both measures should be basic parts of a department's evaluation practices, I have doubts that faculty members or departments are willing to make the commitment that goes with doing them well.

Toward a More Objective Review of Teaching

Regardless of the kind and quality of the somewhat objective data about teaching, those data must be translated into the decisions about retention, promotion, and tenure that peers make. So long as the discussion and vote on retention, promotion, and tenure by one's peers remain essential to the reward system, that long will the efforts to obtain precise and fair data be qualified by the individual opinions and votes of the faculty.

Though some ingenious schemes have appeared here and there to temper this aspect of peer judgment, few attempts have been made to take a big and obvious step. This step is to have a body of disinterested but knowledgeable persons, divorced from personal or even professional acquaintance with the individual, pass judgment upon the data presented, somewhat as reviewers of fellowships and grant applications reach their decisions. Though I do not see faculty members welcoming further complications in an already complicated system, I think the addition of some form of outside judgment is the only way of substantially improving peer review.

Clearly it is conceivable that, within a university, a fair member of responsible faculty panels could be formed, given data carefully compiled to shield the identity of the person, and asked to render a judgment and recommendation on the basis of a department's (or college's or university's) criteria and consonant with the purpose of the review. Such judgments could be made of any or all aspects of faculty performance. What weight such a panel's recommendations would carry within the system would be a point of great contention. Clearly the panel would need to be more than advisory; it might well carry equal weight with the faculty's judgment at the first level of review (Gustad, 1961).

As regards teaching specifically, an outside panel might both review data and make independent observations of teaching, though the difficulties of doing the latter do not make it a likely option. Better by far would be (1) the use of student evaluations as part of the data and (2) panels whose members were thoroughly familiar with what student evaluations can disclose and who would follow strict guidelines in admitting and interpreting data for all faculty reviewed. In addition, this panel would use the teaching files I previously mentioned as the other basis for reaching judgment, and it would adopt whatever procedures were possible and necessary to shield the identity of the person under review.

Such a proposal as I have sketched above would undoubtedly meet strong faculty opposition. Where it might gain support, it would still entangle faculty in exhausting debate on almost every point: How are panels to be picked and who is to pick them? Can anonymity really be preserved? What is to protect the faculty member from the department's inadequate data? Who adjudicates when a panel's views are at odds with a department's? The same kinds of questions were raised and continue to be raised about every aspect of the present system; yet answers were found and are incorporated in the policies and procedures that now govern efficiently operating systems. I see no overpowering pratical obstacles to bringing such a review as I am proposing under acceptable statements of policy and procedures. Moreover, such outside reviewing might be accomplished within a college or university at no net increase in faculty involvement. Rather, time expended less fruitfully in visiting colleagues and in the anxiety-producing discussions that follow would be shifted to a more effective form of participation at the first level of peer review.

I would not seriously bring forth the above proposal if twenty-five years of experience had not acquainted me with the force of prejudice, personal friendships and antagonisms, laziness and inattention, hearsay and rumor, and the rest in the judgments of colleagues about such a personal activity as teaching. Nor do I think the introduction of outside peer review would work in all kinds of institutions or necessarily produce magnificent results in any of them. Still, I have been haunted by the recurring thought that, given the information departments collect, a group of citizens chosen at random from the telephone directory could arrive at better judgments than come out of some department review meetings.

I hasten to add that I am not altogether negative about the workings of the present system. Some of a faculty's disappointments with the system must be lived with because it is an imperfect human system. Indeed, despite grievances and anecdotes about what goes on in secret sessions and despite the occasional litigation, I think the system errs most often on the side of benevolence, that it permits soft judgments rather than harsh. Administrators are frequently critical of the faculty's inability to make tough decisions, to deny tenure to its incompetents. The charge may be true, but the tempering of rigorous professional judgments made along rather narrowly defined lines may in the end provide more total faculty energy for teaching and more breadth than a teaching faculty might otherwise have.

Important Practices in Peer Review

The basic difficulty of supporting peer review and yet seeing in it an element of subjectivity that can subvert the best aims of the system leaves me pessimistic about much actual improvement in the reward system. One side of me entertains a liking for getting rid of all systems and reverting back to the single autocratic judgment that says this one stays and this one goes (Southern Regional Education Board, 1977). (Ideally, this should be made by the wisest individual on campus; short of that and in keeping with democratic principles, each year a single judge might be chosen by lot.) Another side tells me that there has been some progress in evaluating faculty just within the twenty-five years I have been participating in the process. This side enjoins me to draw together from the foregoing discussion some of the practices I think most important in making the best of a peer review system.

Expectations and criteria for retention, promotion, and tenure should be set forth in writing at all levels, in specific terms, and periodically reviewed. Faculty are responsible for seeing that administrators maintain such documents and have them periodically reviewed, and faculty members should be the principal but not the only contributors to such documents.

The diverse services that are vital parts of a department's (or college's or university's) functioning must be defined and valued by the faculty.

The documentary basis for evaluating teaching should depend principally on well-conceived and consistently maintained student evaluations and on a dossier of those materials and statistical data that represent in detail the individual's teaching and teaching-related activities.

At the first level of review, *faculty peers should be engaged as reviewers not only in the usual departmental review bodies but as members of outside panels deliberately operating to afford maximum anonymity and objectivity in the judgments reached.* Such judgments should go directly to the next higher level of review and have equal weight with department judgments.

As this chapter has only touched upon the complexities of the subject, so these suggestions leave out much that is important to peer evaluation. Data are still gathered in a casual way; student evaluation instruments vary widely and change often; other instruments scarcely exist as part of reliable or carefully followed procedures; creditable records of an individual's teaching and accompanying materials are often not available. As a final suggestion consistent with this chapter's emphasis on outside review, all of the practices and procedures, including written documents and instruments used to collect data, should be periodically reviewed by outside professional reviewers. Within the literature of educational evaluation and embodied in practices in some institutions are many means of improving peer evaluation—the bigger need is to get the faculty to make use of them.

Here, I think, the failing is not only with the faculty but with the administration—chairpersons, principally, but also deans and academic vice-presidents—among whose chief responsibilities and competencies should be that of educating and inducing the faculty members to carry out *their* responsibilities. O'Connell and Wergin's opening chapter stressed the critical role that administrators must play, and John Bevan has similarly emphasized the crucial role of chairpersons in the intimately related acts of evaluation and faculty development. Chairpersons and deans exercise considerable power in decisions reached about retention, promotion, and tenure, though such power has probably diminished in the last two decades and is currently to be found more in small institutions than in large ones. Among matters lying outside peer review that need attention if the reward system is to be improved is the development of chairpersons and deans who imaginatively and effectively carry out their responsibilities not only for evaluating but also for developing faculty.

References

Centra, J. A. *Determining Faculty Effectiveness.* San Francisco: Jossey-Bass, 1979.

Ericksen, S. C. "The Dimensions of Merit." *Memo to the Faculty,* No. 61. Ann Arbor: University of Michigan, 1978.

French-Lazovik, G. "Peer Review: Documentary Evidence in the Evaluation of Teaching." In J. Millman (Ed.), *Handbook of Teacher Evaluation.* Beverly Hills, Calif.: Sage, 1981.

Gustad, J. W. *The Career Decisions of College Teachers.* Atlanta, Ga.: Southern Regional Education Board, 1960.

Gustad, J. W. *Policies and Practices in Faculty Evaluation.* Washington, D.C.: American Council on Education, 1961.

Knapper, C. K., Geis, G. L., Pascal, C. E., and Shore, B. M. (Eds.). *If Teaching Is Important . . . The Evaluation of Instruction in Higher Education.* Toronto: Clarke, Irwin, 1977.

Levenstein, A. (Ed.). *Collective Bargaining and the Future of Higher Education: Proceedings of the 5th Annual Conference.* New York: City University of New York, 1977.

McKeachie, W. "Student Rating of Faculty: A Reprise." *Academe: Bulletin of the AAUP,* 1979, *65,* 384–397.

Mason, H. L. *College and University Government: A Handbook of Principles and Practice.* New Orleans, La.: Tulane University, 1972.

Report of the Task Force on Teaching Evaluation at the University of California. Berkeley: University of California, 1980.

Seldin, P. *Successful Faculty Evaluation Programs.* Crugers, N.Y.: Coventry, 1980.

Southern Regional Education Board (SREB). *Faculty Evaluation for Improved Learning.* Atlanta, Ga.: SREB, 1977.

Kenneth E. Eble is professor of English at the University of Utah. His writings on higher education began with The Profane Comedy: American Higher Education in the Sixties *for Macmillan in 1962; his last two books for Jossey-Bass were* The Art of Administration *(1978) and* The Craft of Teaching *(1976).*

*With disturbing frequency, . . . criticism of
evaluation and due process in the academy is
challenging its independence.*

Academic Evaluation
and Due Process

Irwin H. Polishook

The academic enterprise, the fundamental mission of the university, is
greatly influenced by the search and appointment process, by the institution's remuneration structure, and by other methods of professional
recognition and advancement. But its foundation depends largely on the
judgments that come from the evaluation of individual professors. Evaluation and the uses made of evaluation shape the ultimate quality of an
institution's faculty.

No effort is made in this chapter to include the role of nonpedagog-
ical personnel in the evaluation process. Constraints of space require a
limited focus on the professoriate. Much of this commentary, however, is
also applicable to nonclassroom professionals, especially librarians and
counselors.

The desirability of due process in the evaluation of college teachers
is universally accepted. Due process assures the efficiency of the procedure
and the fair treatment of its subjects. The individual teacher, the faculty at
large, the institution, and, indeed, the society of which it is part share a
common concern for the effective and fair judgment of the instructor in
higher education.

Yet, while they share this general consensus, all of those entities
have their own interests in the evaluation sequence. Those interests are

G. French-Lazovik (Ed.). *New Directions for Teaching and Learning:
Practices that Improve Teaching Evaluation*, no. 11. San Francisco: Jossey-Bass, September 1982.

not identical and some are antithetical to others. The individual professor, for example, has an abiding concern for protection against the abuse or misuse of evaluation. The institution has an overriding interest in the development of the faculty. The faculty has a predominant need to foster the primacy and the quality of peer review. The society at large, in turn, balances its interest in institutional excellence with a pervasive concern for individual rights.

Despite what may be characterized as a consensus of values and expectations, evaluation and due process in the American university are elements of an academic system whose internal tensions are frequently overlooked. Conflicts among the constituent bodies of the university have confounded the evaluation process, occasionally impaired its purposes, and even discredited the academy in the public eye. This dysfunction makes it worthwhile to take a closer look at the way various segments of the university community relate to evaluation, and to identify the potential for incongruence within the system's operation. Concentration on these problems can lead to the strengthening of the American university in the decade of the 1980s.

The Individual's Interest

The college professor has three major concerns with the evaluation process: (1) from the constructive commentary that issues from it, the teacher learns how to improve professional performance; (2) its judgments represent the estimation of one's closest academic peers; and (3) from its use, abuse, or misuse, the evaluation influences a person's entire career.

The improvement of performance can be, and is often professed to be, an extremely valuable outcome of the evaluation procedure. It is a systematic means by which professors are reviewed by those presumably qualified to offer the most searching criticism of professional attainment. Working optimally, this procedure identifies the instructor's strengths and affirms the individual's own convictions, which may be vague, about what is being done well. It also identifies weaknesses, citing flaws in performance that mar a professor's effectiveness and that may continue to do so unless overcome. This function of evaluation produces concrete suggestions for the enhancement of the professor's contribution to the university.

When properly carried out, constructive evaluation is of great benefit to the faculty member. It is important in itself and all the more significant in the absence of any other continuous means of professional assistance. Though professors learn a good deal from mentors, colleagues, and publishers about the quality of their research and scholarship, that kind of feedback is problematical, and it is always too much conclusive—yes or no, publishable or not publishable—rather than instructive. In addition, though there are informal ways to gauge the response of students to teaching effectiveness, this uncertain evidence cannot compare to the organized means by which departmental colleagues measure teaching quality. Whatever its particular format, an institutionalized evaluation provides the only systematic review of a professor's total academic performance (Dressel, 1976; Seldin, 1980; Tucker, 1981).

The faculty member's interest in what has been termed "formative" evaluation is of special relevance to this discussion (Centra, 1979; French-Lazovik, 1976). Given the commitment that leads people into academic life, they have a normally healthy concern with the perfection of their professional capability. Rigorous evaluation is a common instrument of professional growth in the academy.

This function of evaluation is often obscured, however, because it is tied to—if not subordinated by—what is called the "summative" purposes of evaluation. No matter what the stated professions of the faculty manual or the faculty contract are and no matter how much lip-service is paid to the goal of improving performance, the constructive critique of professional capacities can be undermined by its judgmental aspect. The evaluation procedure as an end product is designed to measure the professor's worth to the institution—not merely potential worth and individual progress, but the individual's worth at a specific point in time. That rating, the "bottom line," usually forms the basis for the decision that follows on whether or not to reappoint, to grant tenure, or to promote at a particular date. It is virtually impossible for any individual to disregard this aspect of institutional life.

A graphic illustration is seen in a professor's reaction to classroom observations when they are used to measure teaching competence (Seldin, 1980). If the primary purpose of the observation were formative (namely, to improve the teacher's classroom technique), professors would welcome a visit to the most typical sessions with students or perhaps the most routine classroom recitations. Faculty might also seek observations that were unscheduled, random, and impromptu, and probably more than one; the greater the sampling, the better. But that is not usually the case. Wherever classroom visitations are part of the evaluation system, the teacher is inclined to insist on prescheduled observations for which preparations might be made, and inevitably the students are subtly prepared for the exercise, perhaps on a slice of instruction that a teacher feels most comfortable with. Thus, what is subjected to observation is not necessarily typical; the exercise may in extreme cases constitute a departure from the general classroom experience. Whatever conclusions are drawn from this possibly limited focus, the "sample" may have only a tangential connection to the professor's normal performance. Under these circumstances, even direct classroom observations have only marginal utility over less structured ways to judge the quality of university teaching.

Nevertheless, it would be insensible to blame the faculty member for arranging an observation to attain the highest ratings. A professor cannot be expected to play the game of "improvement of performance" alone, that is, to accept the observation of a typical class when other colleagues are able to control the conditions under which their classes are reviewed. Faculty members realize that the process of evaluation is not entirely constructive; its major function in most colleges is to judge an individual's claim to academic preferment. Nor can we blame the professor for calculating that, under such a system, the most urgent objective is survival; those who are deemed inadequate do not remain within the academic community. Permanence depends on the conclusions derived from evaluations—especially those that came first—rather than on the improvement that is demonstrable at some future time.

This is, of course, symptomatic of the problems involved in any form of evaluation. Distortions arise in every method of measuring teaching performance. The degree to which the protective reaction of professors distorts the process depends on the balance maintained between the use of evaluation for the improvement of performance and its place in decisions relating to reappointment and promotion. The university has an obligation to clarify the value given to the results of evaluation if faculty members are to believe they have been treated fairly.

The Institution's Interest

The institution's primary interest in the evaluation process is in its use as a vehicle for the selection of the professional staff. That end is achieved through the use of the formative content of the evaluation (by improving the performance of incumbent personnel) and through the application of summative evaluation to decisions about faculty advancement.

Clearly, the university benefits from the proper working of staff improvement (Astin and Lee, 1967; Miller, 1972). Each faculty appointment represents a considerable institutional investment in the resources required to search for and to select new personnel. In each year of the appointment, that investment is expanded by the institution's expenditures in perfecting the human resource; the evelation procedure itself is a costly operation. All things being equal, it is more cost-efficient to bring an incumbent up to optimum proficiency than to replace a person with a largely unknown quantity. Academic excellence, as a goal of institutional policy, is fostered by evaluation and diluted by the regular turnover of the existing faculty.

The institution acts on the contingency that most appointments will not take hold. It builds into the staff-improvement operation the judgmental design that can be antithetical to it. The same process by which faculty may be improved is the vehicle by which faculty may be removed. The measurement inherent in evaluation may outweigh its developmental purposes, and what the faculty member is, now, may overshadow what the professor may someday become.

From the institution's point of view, due process is primarily a means of efficiency rather than of reasonableness. As a humane institution, the university aspires to fairness in its dealings with personnel, probably more than a commercial business might, and due process assures that fairness (McCarthy, 1981). But it goes beyond that. By conforming to basic principles of evidence in determining the subject's quality, by allowing the individual to participate in the common effort to reach an accurate appraisal, by attempting to guard against the unreliability and refractions of subjectivity, due process assures an accurate conclusion. If the judgment is not accurate, then the retention and advancement decisions flowing from it will be misinformed, and the purpose of improving the staff through intelligent selection will be compromised.

When fairness comes into conflict with the institution's authority to exercise its judgment, due process is sometimes sacrificed. As soon as the university "knows" that an employee is unlikely to be retained, for example, it will attempt to effect a termination despite the contrary evidence that may emerge from evaluation. Many adversary proceedings such as appeals, grievances, and litigation, spring from this inclination.

The institution has one further interest in due process, which lies in the autonomy the institution claims over its own governance. That autonomy, desirable as it is, is not absolute. It is granted and it is suffered for as long as it is exercised to the satisfaction of those whom the university serves. When an alleged violation of due process comes to light, when it is publicized, protested, and challenged, the institution's autonomy is threatened. It is in the interest of the university to avert such threats to its autonomy by the proper working of due process in the evaluation structure.

The Faculty's Interest

The faculty as a whole has interests similar to those of the institution, but its concern over outside interference is not so much directed at the off-campus intrusions. They are the problem of the institution, which must answer and bear the brunt of external criticism, even when the target may be the practice of the faculty itself.

The faculty's major interest is the peer review process: its integrity and the assurance of its effectiveness. This process is essential if academic decisions are to reflect the judgments of scholars, which in turn is central to the quality of any university. Nor does this focus ignore the fact that the faculty's "governance" of the university manifests itself in other areas, especially in the shaping and control of the curriculum, the establishment of requirements for degrees, and the formulation of policies relating to student admission, attendance, grades, and retention. But there is no more important means for faculty to improve the academic enterprise than through its involvement in the selection of its own members (McConnell and Mortimer, 1971; Polishook, 1977). The faculty guards that responsibility with special zeal.

This is why professors claim the right to implement the procedures under which their colleagues are evaluated. They actually conduct the teaching and scholarly appraisals and prepare the evaluations; they also want to assign whatever weight is attached to judgments from other sources, whether faculty outside the institution or students within; and they bear responsibility for whatever faculty-improvement efforts result from the evaluation process. It is their scrupulous recommendations that they expect will prevail whenever reappointments, tenure, and promotions are finally determined.

Other institutional entities also participate in the decision-making process. The college president or chancellor, as the chief academic officer, is either a participant in the faculty peer review procedure, personally or through a designee, or may exercise final approval rights over the recommendation that comes out of peer review. Additionally, the institution's board of trustees generally assumes the authority to pass on the recommendations coming from the chief academic officer who acts in concert with or separate from the faculty.

Whatever the professed roles of the chief academic officer and the board of trustees and no matter how explicitly the institution's policy assigns to either or both of those entities the full authority to overturn or veto the recommendations of the faculty, the faculty members themselves see the function of those bodies as essentially passive. Professors will invariably be offended by wholesale reversals of their own personnel recommendations. Some of the most disruptive and vocal disputes in higher education have been inspired by the exercise of the chief academic officer or the board of trustees of its prerogatives in making the final determination on faculty (Coughlin, 1978; "Court Conditionally Orders," 1980; Jones, 1973).

Challenges to peer review come from other sources. Students, in an organized way, may claim a greater say than they enjoy in the evaluation process (Centra, 1979; Doyle, 1975). Students rarely voice protests about the advancement of faculty members, but they do demand a student evaluation system where it does not exist. Where such a system is in place, they may ask that more weight be attached to it. They covet a participatory role on faculty personnel committees. In less organized ways, students sometimes protest negative decisions on faculty members they consider good teachers.

The faculty member, of course, can challenge such decisions. The individual may utilize an appeal procedure that is built into the peer review process and, if that fails or if an adequate appeal recourse outside a department is unavailable, he or she may initiate an internal grievance if that is possible. With greater frequency professors also "go public," or resort to legal action.

The vulnerability of the faculty to such challenges stems from what professors hold to be the greatest strength of peer review: its integrity as a searching and reasonable process. The structure of the evaluation procedure is occasionally spelled out and the criteria for academic judgments may be delineated. Though far from universal, these are positive practices that are compatible with due process in the academy. Yet, even where elements of fair play are in place, conflicts arise within the very nature of peer review. One grave source of controversy is the amount of secrecy required to promote the most effective judgments by professors of the competence of their colleagues, entailing for tenure decisions a sequence that extends for an average of seven years. It is usual to label this secrecy "confidentiality," although the scope of confidentiality as the word is used infers much more than simply the privacy required to make academic judgments.

Faculty members themselves are confused over what confidentiality requires. Most professors cherish confidentiality because it permits them to make negative personnel decisions as part of a committee without betraying their individual positions or having individual participants openly challenge the academic consensus. In light of this, it is easy to understand why faculty members believe that the secrecy implicit in confidentiality is essential. Insofar as every negative decision is unpopular, then at least one person who normally has served for years as a colleague finds the mantle of confidentiality reassuring. As a result, while the final disposition of peer review bodies is invariably made known at some point, the votes are not divulged, and only rarely are the votes of individual members of faculty bodies polled. More importantly,, it is uncommon for candidates to be given the reasons for a negative academic judgment. Additionally, it is rare that procedures are in place for appeals beyond administrative bodies within the institution. This broad concept of what confidentiality entails is virtually antithetical to society's ideas about due process.

It is no exaggeration to note that discord within the university is generated by the blanket of so-called "confidentiality" as demanded by academic management. Among the arguments used in defense of this system is the claim that it would be difficult to enlist the participation of

94

faculty members in the process if confidentiality were breached and that, once enlisted, it might impede the exercise of critical judgments if faculty decisions were subject to the mandates of due process. Indeed, for some professors the argument takes on the flavor of an ideological proposition, in which confidentiality is defended as inseparable from peer review, which some assert is itself the only due process needed in the academy. This notion of confidentiality encompasses far more than the privacy professors need to secure freedom from coercion in the peer review process.

Actually, the broad assertion of confidentiality aggravates the suspicious reception accorded some negative personnel actions. To those convinced of the worth of the faculty member denied reappointment, absolute confidentiality raises virtually unanswerable questions about the legitimacy of the whole procedure and especially of its failure to afford the individual due process. A crucial issue that is inseparable from the blanket application of confidentiality to all academic decisions is the problem of reasons: why should a professor, who wants to know, not be told the reasons for a negative personnel decision? At one time very few universities gave reasons, maintaining that such a bar of silence was better for the candidate. A policy statement adopted by one university in 1967 asserted that the giving of reasons "is really not in the best interest of the candidate himself, for it makes a matter of record a negative evaluation which may come back to plague him later" ("Personnel and Budget Procedures," 1967, p. 3). Coming at the point at which the institution has decided against the continuance of a faculty member, expressions of solicitude toward the person are hardly convincing. Similarly, assurances that due process was honored under the shadow of absolute confidentiality rest at the level of outright obfuscation of the decision-making process.

In the absence of due process, the faculty is bound to expend its energy on intrainstitutional controversies growing out of negative decisions on appointments, tenure, and promotion. Individual faculty members are prompted to devote inordinate amounts of time protecting confused principles of confidentiality against attacks from their colleagues, other collegiate entities, including students, and outside society. The academy's personnel structure is threatened as long as at its base are restraints that reach beyond what is reasonable and necessary to secure the integrity of peer review.

Society's Interest

Society's interest in due process is inseparable from its general interest in higher education. Almost twelve million people are now enrolled in American colleges and universities. An additional twenty million citizens have received college degrees since 1945. Add to these individuals their families, and add to them the families of those who expect to attend college in the future, and there is a "constituency" for higher education that is exceeded by no other national institution except the public schools.

The interest of that body of people extends beyond their personal experience on campus. It encompasses a healthy appreciation of the importance of higher education as a national resource. That appreciation has its ups and downs, but it is abiding. It is reflected in the coverage of the academy by the media, which, quantitatively, is substantial.

This popular interest in higher education is not matched by accurate perceptions of how the institution works. Tenure itself is widely misperceived. Some take it to be a "lifelong guarantee" of employment regardless of institutional needs, professional performance, or student enrollment. The retrenchment of college professors that mars our current era is tragic proof that tenure does not mean permanence beyond the financial ability and programmatic needs of any university (Brown and Finkin, 1978; Furniss, 1977; Furniss, 1978). On the other hand, the relatively long and demanding process by which tenure is achieved is considered oppressive as compared to the procedure of gaining job security in other occupations; the very term *nonreappointment*, as it is applied to nontenured personnel, is widely misapprehended as a quaint euphemism for firing.

Similar misconceptions obscure the public's understanding of other academic phenomena, like faculty workloads and peer reviews. Knowledge of the academy is clouded even among college-educated populations.

There is one principle that the academic community has succeeded in elucidating to the public at large, thanks to the longstanding efforts of the American Association of University Professors (1977), and that is academic freedom. An acceptance of this tradition, with its correlative compulsion against outside interference, has restrained public opinion from working its will upon the academy directly.

Society's influence on higher education is exercised mostly through government. The courts adjudicate the protection of individual rights that is provided in the Constitution and the laws of the land, and campuses are not immune to their jurisdiction. The federal executive branch enforces these laws and has done so more aggressively since the national investment in higher education has expanded. Among the best known of the strings attached to public funds given to the academy, especially since the Nixon administration, has been affirmative action, primarily in execution of Title VII of the Civil Rights Acts of 1964 and 1972 (Bickel and Brechner, 1978; Kaplin, 1978; Lester, 1979). Regardless of President Reagan's success in reducing federal regulation of the academy, the university will remain subject to the scrutiny of municipal, state, and national governments.

A Case of Conflict

The most dramatic single instance of the academy's vulnerability to society's interest in due process is the celebrated case of Dr. James A. Dinnan ("Academic Freedom vs. Affirmative Action," 1980; Nielsen and Polishook, 1981, "Rights in Conflict," 1981).

Professor Dinnan refused—and was fined and jailed for refusing—to divulge his votes on a faculty committee at the University of Georgia that denied promotion and tenure to Dr. Maija Blaubergs. Professor Blaubergs filed a suit against the university charging sex discrimination and successfully petitioned the court for information about the faculty ballots. The federal judge hearing the case was incensed by Dinnan's recalcitrance. Without betraying sensitivity to the mores of the academy, particularly peer review, the judge denounced the entire system of faculty appointments as violating due process. He reviled professors who want secrecy as lacking "backbone enough to be counted" (Fiske, 1980; "Growing Row," 1980). This outburst occurred despite the fact that Dinnan's votes were already known, even without his personal testimony. Contemptuous of the university, the judge fined Dinnan and sent him to jail. The University of Georgia failed to support Dinnan and counseled him to give up his defense of what had really become a decision to deny Professor Blaubergs' claim to tenure by the institution's administration.

The Dinnan case raises issues far broader than merely the integrity of peer review. These issues were cogently described by Albert Shanker, president of the American Federation of Teachers, in a column that appeared in *The New York Times* on October 5, 1980:

> Dinnan maintained that the right of professors to recommend who should teach is essential to quality higher education. He said that the integrity of the academic process would be undermined if the confidentiality of the votes were breached. Dinnan believes that a grave threat to academic freedom exists when a judge jails a professor for protecting the process needed to make honest decisions about faculty (Section E, p. 7).

Shanker's recognition of the academy's danger is matched by an understanding that no university can be oblivious to its obligation to offer due process to members of the faculty. "In our universities, as in the rest of society, there are instances of sex discrimination, and they must be opposed," Shanker observed. "But this cannot be attained if there are review procedures which are inadequate and need strengthening, so that candidates for tenure and promotion have confidence in the fairness of university decisions." A similar position was later promulgated by the American Association of University Professors (1980, p. 1), when it noted that the jailing of Dinnan, "which we deplore," masked the "underlying issues" of due process.

There seems little dispute that Professor Dinnan was punished too severely for defending his university. His personal cause was an implacable defense of the rules of the university that demanded absolute secrecy about the deliberations of the personnel committee on which he agreed to serve. But the institution itself could not defend Dinnan against the contempt citation of a federal judge. What the case of Dinnan did not clarify is the entire structure of evaluation under which he participated in a faculty personnel committee. This system did not withstand the intercession of the court, despite the evident hostility of a judge, which victimized Dinnan but not the institution he served honorably. Sadly, there have been only rare instances in the history of higher education in which a university equalled Professor Dinnan's devotion to faculty rights and academic autonomy.

What finally complicates any opinion about Dinnan's case is the implication that there is something to be set right at American colleges. In a letter to the *Chronicle of Higher Education,* Ellen Mattingly (1980), president of the AAUP chapter at the University of Georgia, detailed the inadequacy of due process at her own institution: "Not only are no reasons given to terminated nontenured faculty, but the general area of evaluation of faculty performance is deliberately shrouded in secrecy. Files of annual evaluations of performance by department heads are maintained with no access permitted even to the faculty members evaluated. Salary adjustments resulting from such secret evaluations are virtually immune from any appeal without ever receiving an explanation" (p. 24). Nor is there a general "formulated grievance procedure" at the University of Georgia. A response to Professor Mattingly's letter by a University of Georgia official (Trotter, 1980, p. 25) left unchallenged the substance of her condemnation of the system of personnel judgments at the university.

That system's flaws are as familiar as they are unfortunate. Herein is the heart of the problem. American universities cannot resist external intervention so long as their ways in rendering academic decisions remain questionable. Not only at the University of Georgia but also at many other institutions, the instruments of academic judgment will continue to invite outside intervention that threatens university autonomy (Levenstein, 1981). One is constrained to make this point even while emphasizing that reform of the system can be achieved without undermining its foundation of peer review.

Toward Resolutions

Most faculty are satisfied that the evaluation process is efficacious and geared to the recognition of excellence. On the other hand, professors also realize that there are conflicts among constituent bodies of the university—most frequently with college presidents—that occasionally erupt into spectacular battles over academic decisions. A smaller number of faculty are disturbed about the shortcomings of due process for aggrieved colleagues. Still there are few voices demanding an overthrow of the entire structure. Admittedly, not all conflicts within the process of evaluation are resolvable, nor can the disparate interests of the various participants be brought into perfect harmony. Some commonsense improvements in evaluation and due process suggest themselves as a result of this analysis.

There is a clear need to elevate the constructive function of evaluation and to separate it from the final judgment about members of the instructional staff. Otherwise, the first appraisal tends to be the last, binding opinion. Both thrusts of evaluation are of vital importance, but they are difficult to reconcile in practice. An individual who ingenuously submits to criticism in hope of professional advancement may also create devastating initial impressions that are sometimes insurmountable; such a professor is placed at a great disadvantage during every year of evaluation.

There are other simple steps that might ameliorate the conflicts inherent in the evaluation sequence. For instance, the timetable for the two functions of evaluation could be divided; perhaps the people who supervise the process might be selected by the faculty themselves; and the professor who is subjected to the opinions of his colleagues might be permitted to respond. Overall, a clear difference should be sought in evaluations so that faculty growth and "bottom-line" decisions about a professor's career are each given proper valuation.

The second major change in current practices that would substantially reduce the abrasions resulting from evaluation is the enhancement of due process. Certain features of due process may seem obvious, but they are not universal among American universities. Minimum publicized standards should prevail in every institution about the procedures and general criteria for all types of personnel actions. Openness is a virtue with regard to the rights of faculty involved in peer committees, not only clarifying the secrecy that may be desired in their deliberations and documentation, but also the authority accorded their decisions by university administrators. Most disputes about faculty committees do not involve matters related to confidentiality. The greatest contention comes when the faculty, without prior notice about its rights, finds the university's management unilaterally overturning the considered judgments of peer committees. Professors should know in advance who really has the last word in the university.

Much more important are those elements of due process involving the right of appeal and the issue of reasons. Can any university claim it treats professors fairly unless there is an established procedure for appeal by aggrieved individuals? Within the outside society an appellate structure is seen as essential and effective to the extent that it is impartial; there are those who would require that it also be binding.

The issue of reasons for negative personnel actions is a more complex subject. Without the provision of reasons, an individual has little assurance that university personnel decisions reflect adequate consideration of performance, that they do not infringe on academic freedom, and that they were not based on impermissible grounds including inaccuracy, malice, or bias. Professors who are not told the reasons for negative judgments may very well dispute the value of elaborate evaluations since the data produced can easily have been disregarded. Furthermore, without reasons, it is difficult, if not impossible, to establish outside the university that any particular academic judgment was not arbitrary, unreasonable, or discriminatory. Though most personnel decisions are the product of honest and searching reviews, all of them are suspect in the absence of stated reasons. Reasons would thus strengthen the university and help to secure its autonomy against unwarranted intrusions by government.

If no man is an island, then the American university is surely not a continent. We live in a complex world of expanding societal concepts of individual rights, with greater incentives for individuals to challenge the academy. Professors know that despite its flaws our nation's universities are devoted to excellence and social progress. With disturbing frequency, however, criticism of evaluation and due process in the academy is challenging its independence. A few moderate reforms can enrich the university and generate a greater sense of confidence in its well-being.

References

"Academic Freedom vs. Affirmative Action: Ga. Professor Jailed in Tenure Dispute." *The Chronicle of Higher Education,* September 20, 1980.

American Association of University Professors. "A Preliminary Statement on Judicially Compelled Disclosure in the Nonrenewal of Faculty Appointments." Statement adopted by the Council of the American Association of University Professors, Washington, D.C., November 21, 1980.

American Association of University Professors. *Policy Documents and Reports.* Washington, D.C.: American Association of University Professors, 1977.

Astin, A., and Lee, C. "Current Practices in the Evaluation and Training of College Teachers." In C. Lee (Ed.), *Improving College Teaching.* Washington, D.C.: American Council on Education, 1967.

Bickel, R. D., and Brechner, J. A. (Eds.). *The College Administration and the Courts.* Asheville, N.C.: College Administration Publications, 1978.

Brown, Jr., R. S., and Finkin, M. W. "The Usefulness of AAUP Policy Statement D." *Educational Record,* 1978, *59* (1), 30–44.

Centra, J. A. *Determining Faculty Effectiveness.* San Francisco: Jossey-Bass, 1979.

Coughlin, E. K. "Maryland President Decides Not to Hire Marxist." *The Chronicle of Higher Education,* July 31, 1978, p. 5.

"Court Conditionally Orders College to Award Tenure." *The Chronicle of Higher Education,* March 3, 1980, p. 9.

Doyle, Jr., K. O. *Student Evaluation of Instruction.* Lexington, Mass.: Lexington Books, 1975.

Dressel, P. L. *Handbook of Academic Evaluation.* San Francisco: Jossey-Bass, 1976.

Fiske, E. B. "Jailing of a Professor Heightens Fears for Campus Independence." *New York Times,* September 14, 1980, p. 1.

French-Lazovik, G. *Evaluation of College Teaching.* Washington, D.C.: Association of American Colleges, 1976.

Furniss, W. T. "The 1976 AAUP Retrenchment Policy." *Educational Record,* 1977, *58* (2), 133–139.

Furniss, W. T. "The Status of 'AAUP Policy.'" *Educational Record,* 1978, *59* (1), 7–29.

"Growing Row over 'Peer Review.'" *Time,* October 6, 1980, pp. 78–79.

Jones, L. Y. "Advanced-Study Center Moving to End Dispute with Faculty." *The Chronicle of Higher Education,* April 9, 1973, p. 1.

Kaplin, W. A. *The Law of Higher Education: Legal Implications of Administrative Decision-Making.* San Francisco: Jossey-Bass, 1978.

Lester, R. A. *Anti-bias Regulations of Universities: Faculty Problems and Their Solutions.* New York: McGraw-Hill, 1979.

Levenstein, A. "Confidentiality and Due Process." Newsletter (National Center for the Study of Collective Bargaining in Higher Education and the Professions), 1981, *9* (4), 1–3.

Mattingly, E. "Publicity over Jailed Professor Obscures Problems at U. of Georgia." Letter to the editor. *The Chronicle of Higher Education,* September 29, 1980, p. 24.

McCarthy, J., and Ladimer, I. *Resolving Faculty Disputes.* New York: American Arbitration Association, 1981.

McConnell, T. R., and Mortimer, K. D. *The Faculty in University Governance.* Berkeley: Center for Research and Development in Higher Education, University of California, 1971.

Miller, R. I. *Evaluating Faculty Performance.* San Francisco: Jossey-Bass, 1972.

Nielsen, R. M., and Polishook, I. H. "The Vulnerable Academy." *The Chronicle of Higher Education,* January 19, 1981, p. 9.

"Personnel and Budget Procedures." *Minutes of Proceedings, Board of Higher Education, City of New York.* New York: Board of Higher Education, December 18, 1967, 598–602.

Polishook, I. "Peer Judgment and Due Process." *Collective Bargaining and the Future of Higher Education: Proceedings of the Fifth Annual Conference, National Center for the Study of Collective Bargaining in Higher Education.* New York: National Center for the Study of Collective Bargaining in Higher Education, Baruch College, City University of New York, 1977.

"Rights in Conflict: The Secrecy of the Tenure Vote." Newsletter (National Center for the Study of Collective Bargaining in Higher Education and the Professions), 1981, *9* (5), 1–4.

Seldin, P. *Successful Faculty Evaluation Programs.* Crugers, N.Y.: Coventry, 1980.

Shanker, A. "Prof's Jailing Threatens College Quality." *New York Times,* October 5, 1980, Section E, p. 7.

Trotter, Y. "Promotion, Grievance Policies at the University Of Georgia." Letter to the editor. *The Chronicle of Higher Education,* November 17, 1980, p. 25.

Tucker, A. *Chairing the Academic Department.* Washington, D.C.: American Council on Education, 1981.

Irwin H. Polishook is professor of history of Lehman College, City University of New York, president of the Professional Staff Congress, the union representing the instructional staff of CUNY, vice-president of the American Federation of Teachers, and chairperson of the AFT advisory commission of higher education.

What are some of the signs that sound policies and
due process characterize a teaching evaluation system?

Some Benchmarks of a Teaching Evaluation System for Summative Use

Grace French-Lazovik

This list of benchmarks is presented instead of a summary of the previous chapters. With only a few exceptions, the items on it are taken from the chapters, but their full meaning can be understood and their importance appreciated only by reading what each author has to say.

While its repetition constitutes an embarrassment, nevertheless the overwhelming importance of one principle requires continual emphasis; that principle is that none of these procedures will work unless an institution's administrators are honestly committed to improving the teaching of their faculty through just and humane policies. Nor is that enough; faculty must also be convinced of that commitment.

1. The evaluation procedures and policies must have the support (and during development or revision, the involvement) of top academic administrators.
2. Faculty must have participated, through committees and through general meetings, in the planning of the system, and they must be aware of their impact on the policies developed.
3. Evaluation expertise must be available to help plan, guide, and monitor the system.

G. French-Lazovik (Ed.). *New Directions for Teaching and Learning:*
Practices that Improve Teaching Evaluation, no. 11. San Francisco: Jossey-Bass, September 1982.

4. Teaching should be evaluated separately from other academic responsibilities.

5. Only explicitly stated and performance-relevant criteria should be considered. Essentially this requirement specifies that characteristics unrelated to performance, such as race, sex, or ethnic background, should not enter into the evalution of teaching performance.

6. A clear statement of the procedures and policies that they will follow should be endorsed by all administrators who participate in decisions about faculty performance.

7. A clear description of all aspects of the evaluation system should be communicated to faculty *in writing* at the earliest possible point. Faculty members should know the criteria by which they will be judged, their responsibility in providing dossier materials, and the responsibility and authority of administrators in evaluating faculty performance.

8. Methods of data collection and policies that govern them should be appropriate to the evaluation purpose for which they are used.

9. The evaluation instruments and procedures used should provide data that are reliable, valid, and comparable within academic units if the results are considered in decisions.

10. Policies should apply equally to all faculty members within defined units; that is, they should be nondiscriminatory within units but not necessarily identical across units (the standards and procedures for judging clinical teaching in medicine, for example, may be quite different from those in arts and sciences).

11. Help for an individual faculty member trying to improve his or her teaching must be available.

12. Department chairpersons should be trained in the aspects of their role that involve evaluating faculty members and making recommendations regarding them.

13. On a regular basis (not just at times of academic decisions), feedback from administrators should be given each faculty member in writing, including reasons for decisions or suggestions for improvement. This letter should be accompanied by an interview in which the department chairperson and the faculty member can discuss the evaluation and the faculty member can respond to it.

14. At least two levels of administrative review should assure that published policies have been followed in decisions of appointment renewal or tenure.

15. There should be a clearly defined appeals process.

16. Academic rewards should be tied to evaluation in an equitable way.
17. The evaluation system should take as little faculty time as possible. Thus, budget resources should provide for administrators or administrative units to carry out as much of the data collection, collating, and reporting as possible. Faculty time should be used only where it is essential.
18. A specified group or committee, creditable to faculty and administrators, should periodically review the evaluation system and report publicly on its operation. The frequency of review and the mechanism by which improvements can be introduced should be provided within the initial specifications of policy.

Even though this list concerns evaluation for decisions, good practice recommends that as much formative use of evaluation results as possible be built into the system.

Additional Readings

The research literature on teaching evaluation is voluminous and is found primarily in journals. A few of the most widely available are: *Journal of Educational Psychology, Teaching of Psychology, Journal of Higher Education, American Educational Research Journal,* and *Review of Educational Research.*

The following references provide useful summaries of that literature.

Summaries published before 1975 are:

Eble, K. E. *The Recognition and Evaluation of Teaching.* Washington, D.C.: American Association of University Professors, 1970.
Costin, F., Greenough, W. T., and Menges, R. J. "Student Ratings of College Teaching: Reliability, Validity, and Usefulness." *Review of Educational Research,* 1971, *41,* 511-535.
Miller, R. I. *Developing Programs for Faculty Evaluation.* San Francisco: Jossey-Bass, 1974.

More recent works, published in the last three years, that provide helpful overviews of research findings are:

Centra, J. A. *Determining Faculty Effectiveness.* San Francisco: Jossey-Bass, 1979.
McKeachie, W. J. "Student Ratings of Faculty: A Reprise." *Academe,* 1979, *65,* 384-397.

Millman, J. *Handbook of Teacher Evaluation.* Beverly Hills, Calif.: Sage, 1981.

Seldin, P. *Successful Faculty Evaluation Programs.* Crugers, N.Y.: Coventry, 1980.

Grace French-Lazovik is director of the Office for the Evaluation of Teaching at the University of Pittsburgh. Her work in teaching evaluation began over thirty years ago at the University of Washington with Professor Edwin Guthrie, one of the field's earliest pioneers.

Index

A

Academe, 1–2
Academic evaluation. *See* Faculty evaluation; Peer evaluation; Teaching
"Academic Freedom vs. Affirmative Action," 96, 99
Accountability, and evaluative procedures, 6, 95–96
Administration: centralization of and innovation, 12–13; faculty trust of, 10–11; strategies of for evaluative change, 13–15
Administrative evaluation, 38–39; forms for, 40–41
Administrators: and changing evaluation procedures, 8–9; evaluative priorities of, 4; faculty evaluation concerns of, 6–7
Affirmative action, and faculty evaluation, 6, 95
American Association of University Professors, 34, 95, 97, 99
American Educational Research Journal, 105
Anstey, E., 61, 72
Astin, A., 90, 99

B

Banking of credits, 37–38
Batista, E. E., 65, 72
Bennis, W. G., 17
Berman, P., 10–12, 17
Berne, K. D., 17
Bevan, J. M., 19–43, 78
Bickel, R. D., 95, 99
Blaubergs, M., 96
Blaubergs versus Regents of the University System of Georgia, 67
Bloom, B. S., 58, 72
Bolar, M., 61, 72
Brechner, J. A., 95, 99
Brown, R. S., Jr., 95, 100

C

California, University of at Berkeley, 74–75
Centra, J. A., 1–2, 39, 42, 49, 54, 57, 72, 76, 85, 89, 92, 100, 105
Chin, R., 17
Chronicle of Higher Education, 97
Cohen, P. A., 48, 54, 57, 72
Computerized rating systems, 5
Conrad, C. F., 9, 11, 17
Costin, F., 105
Coughlin, E. K., 92, 100
"Court Conditionally Orders College to Award Tenure," 92, 100

D

Data: for faculty evaluation, 5–6, 16; maintaining of, 80, 84; norm establishment in, 51–52; norm referencing in, 70–71; soundness of, 45–46; from students, policy on, 50–51; from students; quality of, 49–50; from students, use of, 48–49; validity issues in, 63–65; weighting of, 53–54
Deci, E. L., 71–72
Decision making: centralization of an innovation, 12–13; evaluation of, 40
Department chairpersons: and changing evaluation procedures, 16; and effective evaluation, 22–24; evaluation of, 19–20, 38–39; evaluative letter from, 27–29; as Janus figure, 21–22
Dinnan, J. A., 96–97
Docent in teaching position, 37
Doyle, K. O., Jr., 92, 100
Dressel, P. L., 89, 100
Due process issues: conflict over, 96–97; conflict resolution in, 97–99; faculty interest in, 91–94; individual interest in, 88–90; institutional interest in, 90–91; societal interest in, 94–96

Instructional Development and Effectiveness Assessment System (IDEA), 48–49
Interdisciplinary lecturer post, 37

J

Jones, L. Y., 92, 100
Journal of Educational Psychology, 105
Journal of Higher Education, 105

K

Kane, J. S., 67, 72
Kansas State University, 48–49
Kaplin, W. A., 95, 100
Knapper, C. K., 81, 85
Krathwohl, D. R., 58, 72

L

Ladimer, I., 100
Landy, F. J., 67, 72
Lawler, E. F., III, 67, 72
Learning process, and evaluation, 58–60. *See also* Teaching
Lee, C., 90, 99
Lepper, M. R., 71–72
Lester, R. A., 95, 100
Levenstein, A., 77, 85, 97, 100

M

McCarthy, J., 91, 100
McConnell, T. R., 92, 100
McKeachie, W. J., 1–2, 48, 54, 57, 72, 81, 85, 105
Maguire, J. D., 9, 11–12, 17
Masia, B., 58, 72
Mason, H. L., 77, 85
Mattingly, E., 97, 100
Mayhew, L. B., 9–13, 17
Menges, R. J., 105
Michigan, University of, 74–75
Miller, R. I., 9–10, 12, 17, 65, 72, 90, 100, 105
Millman, J., 42, 54, 72, 85, 106
Mohrman, K., 42
Morgan, G. A., 20, 42
Mortimer, K. D., 92, 100

N

New York Times, 96, 101
Nielsen, R. M., 96, 100
Northwestern University, 49

O

O'Connell, W. R., Jr., 3–17, 42, 47, 54, 84–85

P

Pascal, C. E., 85
Pauley, E., 10–12, 17
Peer evaluation: colleagueship and, 65; confidentiality issues in, 93–94, 96–97; conflict of interest in, 65; criticisms of, 78–79, 92; due process and anonymity of, 67; effectiveness of, 61–65; faculty role and responsibility in, 79–80, 91–94; forms for, 69; important practices in, 83–85; issues and controversies of, 65–67; minimizing effort in, 68–70; qualifications issues in, 60–61; recommendations on, 67–71; right to, 76–77; selection of raters for, 64, 66–67; structure of, 80–81; subjective judgments in, 80–81
"Personnel and Budget Procedures," 94, 100
Polishook, I. H., 87–101
Pressman, J., 12–13, 17
Promotion: decisions on, 29–36, 53; due process issues in, 90–92

R

Rand Corporation, 10–12
Reagan, R., 95–96
Report of the Task Force on Teaching Evaluation at the University of California, 85
Research, faculty attitudes towards, 74–75, 78
Research awards, 37
Research resources fellow, 36–37
Review of Educational Research, 105
"Rights in Conflict: The Secrecy of the Tenure Vote," 96, 100

110